BLOOD MONEY . . .

"We have a proposition for you, mister."

The Virginian looked toward the swinging doors of the saloon. Through the doorway he could see the women standing in a tight, silent group. Grief was still plain on every face. But there was also grim determination visible in the eyes and the mouthlines.

The widow of Borderville's druggist stepped across the threshold and walked to where Steele was seated. Then, leaning forward, she upended her carpetbag over the table. Jewelry spilled out, along with bills and coins. Without looking at her, Steele began picking out the bills from the littered table-top, stacking and counting them as she related Sherrill's escape.

"The men attempted to take him from the jail-house and string him up. Only Sheriff Brown prevented it. Even now, after what happened yesterday, we're grateful to the sheriff for his stand. At least our menfolk died without the sin of a lynchin' weighin' on their conscience."

"How about your conscience, ladies?" Steele asked levelly. "No sin to pay a man two hundred and thirty-one dollars to do your killing for you?"

"The jewelry will fetch better than two thousand, we figure," the widow rasped. "And we'll do our own dirty dishes, mister. Just need you to gather them up for us." She waved a hand over the table. "This is for expenses while you hunt them down. Sherrill and his thugs emptied the bank. You can keep every cent they ain't spent. All you got to do is bring them back. . . ."

THE ADAM STEELE SERIES:

No. 13
George G. Gilman

ADAM STEELE
BLOODY BORDER

PINNACLE BOOKS ● LOS ANGELES

STEELE #13:   BLOODY BORDER

Copyright © 1977 by George G. Gilman

First published in Great Britain by
New English Library Ltd., 1977

A Pinnacle Books edition, published by special
arrangement with New English Library Ltd.
First printing, April 1979

ISBN: 0-523-40523-5

Cover illustration by Fred Love

Printed in the United States of America

PINNACLE BOOKS, INC.
2029 Century Park East
Los Angeles, California 90067

for Mike, who made one wedding
particularly white!

CHAPTER ONE

Borderville had the appearance of a new ghost town as Clyde Sherrill looked down upon it from the vantage point of a hilltop. But the pleasant tones of a well-tuned pump-organ and its melodious accompaniment of many voices raised to sing a popular hymn betrayed the visual lie.

It was a two-street town, laid out in the form of a V. The church was sited at the meeting point of the two streets at the southern end of town and was the closest building to the watcher on the hill crest. Like almost every other building in Borderville, it was constructed of adobe. Only the Far West Saloon on Main Street and the courthouse on Mine Road were built of expensively imported timber. These were also the only two-story buildings in town. As if the material of their construction and the style of their architecture were not enough to stress the town's attempt to show it was American despite its obvious Mexican beginnings, both the saloon and the courthouse displayed the stars and stripes at the head of roof-mounted flagpoles.

The flags hung limp in the still, cooling air of Sunday evening. West-facing windows reflected the reddening light of the sinking sun. Long shadows thrown eastward were already as dark as approaching night and looked as if they would be cold to sit in.

"Fine-lookin' town for someone who ain't got no bad memories of it, Mr. Sherrill."

1

For part of a second, the man astride the black stallion was startled. For less than two minutes he had remained erect in the saddle, his eyes fixed upon the small town—no line of his expression revealing the depth and scope of his thoughts.

"It's still a fine-looking place, Thad," he growled, instantly controlling the anger which the man's interruption had aroused in him. Hatred showed on his face then, but not for the man. He shifted his gaze back toward Borderville and spat. The ball of moisture arced high over the stallion's head and hit the ground ten feet away. The dusty slope accepted the water thirstily. "It's the men that live there make me feel sick to my stomach."

Sherrill was forty-two and carried his age well. He was six feet tall and several pounds underweight. The black pants and gray shirt he wore had been purchased before he had shed the flesh and now looked baggy on him. The bone structure of his bare hands and face was clearly defined by the slack flesh. His features had always been angular and this was emphasized now, at the forehead, jaw and cheeks. There was an underplayed handsomeness in his face, due mainly to the clear blueness of his deep-set eyes and the pleasant line of his full mouth. It was these two features which contributed to his youthful appearance, and even a two-day growth of thick, black bristles could not detract from this. When he removed his hat and used the back of his hand to wipe the last of the day's sweat from his forehead, he showed a head of black, short-cropped hair. His complexion was deeply bronzed by a lifetime's exposure to every extreme of the weather.

"You looked at it long enough, Mr. Sherrill?"

Thadius Bergen was twenty. Fat and soft from working only at making other men work. Just as the older man's clothing hung on a bony frame, so Bergen's shirt and pants tightly contoured his bulges of fat. The

2

youngster had a round face with a snub nose and small eyes. Scars of old acne and the angry red swellings of new outbreaks featured his skin. Rather than bristles, soft down sprouted on his face, blond like the curly hair on his head. It grew thicker along his top lip where he was attempting to cultivate a moustache.

"You anxious to get to the killing?"

As he asked the question, Sherrill turned wearily from the waist and glanced behind him. Eight men looked up at him from a hollow some twenty yards down the slope. All of them were closer to the age of Sherrill than of Bergen. One of them fifty, the rest between thirty-five and forty. One a Mexican, the others American. All as tired and travel-stained as the two on the hill crest. Seven mounted and one on the ground, this last having handed the reins of his horse to a companion while he stood beside a pack animal. This was an unsaddled burro—its burden a corpse sewn into a burlap sack. For more than two days the body had been lashed to the burro but the man on the ground had already cut through the ropes.

"I don't have the impatience of youth no more, Mr. Sherrill. But I sure am anxious to be rid of the judge."

"I think we all feel the same, *señor*," the Mexican said, and the others nodded. "He's really beginning to get up all our noses."

Only the Mexican grinned. Most of the others grimaced. The man closest to the putrid corpse continued to express eagerness, and rasped the Bowie knife over the bristles of his jawline.

Sherrill breathed in deeply through his nose. The leading arc of the crimson sun had touched the highest ridges of the mountains to the west and he was now conscious of the evening chill. The stink of decomposed flesh was not so pungent as it had been throughout the blisteringly hot day, but it was still strong enough to spread a grimace of distaste across his gaunt face. Dur-

3

ing the brief period he had surveyed the town and allowed his mind to conjure up old memories, he had been totally unaware of his immediate surroundings and the component parts. Which was why he had experienced a stab of self-anger when young Thad Bergen made him aware he had dropped his guard against the present as he reflected on the past.

The hymn singing ended in the church. A final note sounded from the organ and then there was silence. Sherrill looked down toward Borderville again and guessed Preacher Dorcas was leading the congregation in prayer. But the voices, reverently hushed, did not carry out of the slit windows in the adobe and over the quarter-mile distance to where Sherrill and Bergen sat their stallions.

"Cut him out and tie him on, Wheeler," Sherrill instructed and did not turn around as the men in the hollow made sounds of relief and approval.

Instead, he shifted his gaze from left to right and then altered the focus of his eyes to peer due north, beyond the town.

The point to where he had ridden forward from the halted group and reined in his mount was at the top of the final northern foothill of the Sierra Madre. Halfway down the slope, which finished at the edge of the tiny graveyard behind the church, was a signpost with two arms. Branded into the sun-bleached timber of the arms were the crudely formed letters to show that the post marked the Sonora-Arizona border: MEXICO to the south and UNITED STATES to the north.

At this point on the international line there was no trail. Where the buildings ended on Mine Road, a trail curved out into some hills in the west, following the line of a dry wash. Sherrill knew it led to the silver-mines, which were the reason for Borderville's existence. The continuance of Main Street was another trail, this one running due north to link with the Gila River Trail.

even though the hymn singing from the church would have masked them. Wheeler Mitchell and the Mexican reined in their horses, dismounted and slid Winchester rifles from the forward-hung saddleboots before hitching the animals to a dusty sycamore tree. As they picked their way between the tombstones of the graveyard, the other riders closed up on Sherrill and the group swung wide to the right. They emerged on to the meeting of the two streets immediately in front of the church.

While Sherrill remained in the saddle, the others dismounted, all of them drawing Winchesters. Again, working to a well-discussed plan, no words were spoken. Thad Bergen gathered the reins of all the unburdened animals and led them along Main Street. By the time he had hitched them to the rail outside the Far West Saloon and returned to where Sherrill waited, the other men had gone from sight.

He knew where they were. Tom Kastle and Charlie Pike were on the roof of the Borderville Bank, a triangular building immediately opposite the church. Vince Bowton and Matt Webb were in Preacher Dorcas's house which was the first building on the east side of Main Street. Phil Riley and John Slade occupied the stage-depot which was across the fork of the two streets, on the west side of Mine Road.

The youngster seemed about to say something to the leader of the intruders, but Sherrill spoke first.

"Last verse, boy." The expression of his gaunt face was grave and his tone was flat. "Best you hurry."

"I don't like it you bein' out here in the open, sir." Bergen's concern sounded in his tone and could be seen on his blotched and scarred face.

"Shoot straight and think of now," Sherrill advised. "But remember that past. Wasn't one man I trusted in the group who got killed. Likewise, I came through."

Bergen nodded emphatically, then whirled and ran

7

toward the church. It was built sideways onto the V of the streets. There was a stunted tower at the western end. The arched entrance porch was at the eastern end. A wooden bench enabled Bergen to climb easily onto the roof of the porch.

When the youngster was in position, Sherrill grunted with satisfaction and nudged his horse forward, angling across to the doorway of the bank which was at the narrowest point of the building. There was a sign jutting out above the door, extending the width of the sidewalk. He untied the drag line from his saddlehorn, stood in the stirrups and reached up to curl the rope around the sign support bracket. Then, with the ease of a man who had strength in reserve, he hauled hand-over-hand on the rope. The naked and mutilated corpse was dragged for a final few feet, then was pulled erect onto the stumps of the ankles. A last jerk lifted it clear of the ground and Sherrill knotted the rope around the bracket.

He drew a knife to cut off the excess length, then sat in his saddle again and eased the stallion away. He halted the animal a hundred feet in front of the church entrance and glanced back toward his handiwork as he dropped the spare rope and sheathed the knife. A narrow line of very white teeth showed in a thin smile. A match flared on the roof of the bank and the dark silhouette of a man suddenly took on the recognizable build and features of Tom Kastle as the flame touched a lamp wick.

The hymn ended and boot leather scraped the floor of the church. Kastle used his Winchester for the additional reach necessary to stretch the lamp over the sidewalk and hook it on the end of the sign bracket. Then, as the cone of light fell over the dead man, brightly illuminating the terrible wounds, Kastle went down into the prone position and was hidden by the roof line of the bank.

A buzz of conversation was coming from the church.

Sherrill shivered once, but not because of the chill air clamped over the town and surrounding desert. It was a tremor of excitement. When it was over, he was rock steady. He made a rest with his left forearm a foot in front of his face, and drew an old Navy Colt from his tied-down holster. He did not cock the action until the barrel was laid against his shirt-sleeve. Then he took slow, careful aim and squeezed the trigger.

The report of the revolver forced a moment of silence into the church. Then the bullet cracked through the timber framework which crowned the short tower and ricocheted with a low-pitched clang against the bell. The thud as it was half buried in a timber strut was swamped by a raucous explosion of vocal sound and heavy footfalls.

By the time the first man lunged out of the church, Sherrill had holstered the Colt and drawn the Winchester from its boot. The action was pumped and the stock plate was hard against his shoulder.

"Evening, Sheriff."

The lawman was sixty with a once-beefy build turned to fat by a life of ease. Hard on his heels as he skidded to a halt was the older Preacher Dorcas in his cleric's robes, two young men who ran the stage depot and the dapper Henry Bloomfield, the bartender at the Far West Saloon.

As they came to an abrupt halt behind the sheriff, Bloomfield snapped his head around to yell into the noisy church.

"It's Clyde Sherrill! With a gun!"

"Dear God in Heaven!" one of the young men croaked, pointing a shaking hand. "Look what he did to Judge King!"

There was silence in the church again. The sheriff and the other young man stared in horror across at the brightly illuminated corpse strung from the bank sign.

9

When Bloomfield turned to look in the same direction his mouth fell open and bright-colored vomit spurted out. He leaned against the porch, then dropped on his haunches and pressed his head down between his knees.

"What's happening?" a woman shrieked from the church as Dorcas stooped at the side of the retching bartender.

"Stay inside!" Sheriff Charlton Brown bellowed, dragging his gaze away from the corpse to stare at Sherrill.

The gaunt-faced, tall man astride the stallion knew the law officer's name. He knew the names of many of the other people forming the congregation. And all their faces, unless there were any strangers in Borderville who had attended church this Sunday evening.

He was not surprised to see that the men outside the porch were dressed in their best suits and did not carry guns. Sherrill's men would not be surprised either, for he had told them how easy it would be.

"I'm not in your jailhouse now, Sheriff," Sherrill said into the silence which Brown's order had produced. "And I've got the gun instead of you this time. I feel that gives me the right to tell you and the rest what to do."

Bloomfield had emptied his stomach and the stench of his fresh vomit was stronger than the sickly sweet odor from the rotting corpse. The preacher helped him to his feet and then, like the two youngsters, both stared at the suspended body out of horror-contorted faces.

"What d'you want, Sherrill?" the lawman asked and waved a pudgy hand toward the corpse in the cone of lamplight. "More of the same kind of vengeance?"

"I want the women and children to stay inside the church, Sheriff. I want all the men outside. Men start at age sixteen."

"What for?"

Sherrill's expression had been impassive since he

10

ended the smile. Now hatred gleamed from his clear blue eyes. "Answered a great many questions in the courthouse of this town—if you recall. I don't intend to answer any more."

He raked the Winchester slightly to the right and squeezed the trigger. The range was fifty feet. The dapper Henry Bloomfield, who had managed to direct his sickness away from his smart suit, expressed mild surprise as the bullet drove into his chest, left of center. An instant later his eyes snapped wider still and his mouth gaped, as if to scream or to spurt more vomit. The lead penetrated his heart and impacted against the inside of his spine. He staggered backward into the porch of three steps and was dead on the third. The death rattle sounded in his throat. He stopped, teetered, then corkscrewed to the ground. In death, he was no longer dapper. Blood oozed from the hole in his chest and blossomed into a large stain.

The sheriff, the preacher and the two men from the stage depot seemed to be carved out of solid marble. Even their skin appeared to be fashioned from the same kind of stone.

"Used to like Henry," Sherrill said flatly, levering the repeater action. "The only bartender I ever met who didn't try to shortchange a drunk. Men outside, women and children in. Now."

"He said now!" Wheeler Mitchell yelled.

"We will kill many loved ones if the order is not obeyed very, very soon!" the Mexican augmented.

Mitchell and Manuel Gomez were still outside the church. But each was at a south-facing window, showing their rifles and their bristled, dust-grimed faces to everyone inside. Some women screamed and some children cried. Men attempted to placate them. But the noise did not end until the sheriff yelled, "Quiet! We got to do what he says!"

11

He spoke the words fast, as Sherrill moved the Winchester again—to draw a bead on the preacher.

"Hurry!" Dorcas urged, springing erect from where he had crouched to mutter a blessing over the body of Bloomfield.

Sherrill's stallion was well schooled to the wants of his rider. A touch on each flank from the man's boot toes caused him to back step for several yards. Across the fork of the two streets until he was level with the suspended corpse. A single, soft-spoken word halted him there.

Men were emerging from the church by then, to the accompaniment of women's sobs and children's wails. The sheriff advanced on Sherrill to clear the porch. The preacher and the two youngsters held back. Those who were first out shuffled forward reluctantly under pressure from those behind them. There was no attempt to escape the open street; rather, the men huddled together as if gaining a degree of comfort from the close proximity of others in the same danger.

Only Sheriff Brown stood lightly apart from the group, grim faced and afraid. The others matched his expression after viewing the body of Judge King with horror then realizing that he was beyond harm while they were not.

Sherrill recognized every face turned toward him from the group of more than fifty frightened men. He made no attempt to match names to them or to distinguish between the twelve who had sat on the jury and those who had formed the lynch mob.

"That's the last of them!" Mitchell called.

The sounds of anguish and terror from the church were subdued now. Then a rifle shot exploded. Something made of glass shattered. An instant of silence was followed by the start of a roar of anger from the townsmen grouped outside.

"Just a warning!" Gomez snarled at the top of his voice. "Nobody is hurt . . . this time!"

Sheriff Brown had halted ten feet in front of the mounted rifleman. He looked beyond the stallion, toward the group of horses hitched outside the saloon.

"Ten of us," Sherrill confirmed. His voice was loud, to capture the attention of the rest of the men, packed into a tight bunch immediately outside the church. Then he lowered his tone but his words could be clearly heard in the otherwise totally silent town. "We went after the judge first. He directed the jury and he pronounced the sentence. I wanted him to suffer badly. Be content just to see the rest of you die."

He squeezed the Winchester's trigger a second time. As before, the stallion did no more than prick his ears at the sound of the gunshot. The bullet drove into Brown's throat and blasted clear at the nape of his neck in a welter of spraying blood. If the lawman made a sound as his mouth gaped as he crumpled, it was swamped by the abrupt disturbance behind him.

Men roared, screamed and cursed. Their feet stomped the hard-packed dirt as they whirled to scatter.

Up on the roof of the bank two men rose erect, light from the lamp above the mutilated corpse shining on their rifle barrels and exposed teeth. Two men lunged out of the preacher's house and two more appeared from the doorway of the stage depot. Thad Bergen went up on to one knee above the church porch.

Sherrill fired again in isolation. Then a fusillade of rifle shots exploded. The town blacksmith took a bullet in the back of his head. Preacher Dorcas had a kneecap shattered, then was holed in the heart as he fell. Three miners went down. The sixteen-year-old son of the town baker was hit twice in the stomach. The banker lost his right eye and experienced an instant of burning agony before the damaging bullet penetrated his brain.

Another volley cut down more men.

13

The two men from the stage depot attempted to find shelter in the church. Thad Bergen shot one in the forehead. Then the second in the back as the man whirled to run away.

None of the killers moved from his position. All merely raked their rifles from left to right, tracking their panicked victims and killing them with cold, relentless ease.

The reports from the rifles of Mitchell and Gomez sounded louder than any others, the explosions amplified by being in a confined space. But they were only warning shots, aimed high across the church and toward the doorway, designed to force the women and children to the floor and dissuade them from attempting to leave.

Outside, on the meeting point of the streets, bodies fell on bodies or sprawled across vacant dirt. The screams of the wounded competed with the yells of terror from those who were still on their feet and fleeing.

But only one man escaped the hail of bullets in front of the church. And he was brought down over a tombstone in the graveyard—shot in the back by the grinning Manuel Gomez.

In less than a minute and a half from the time Sherrill killed the lawman, every male resident of Borderville over the age of sixteen was dead or dying. The intruders closed in then, Bergen dropping down from the porch roof and Kastle and Pike climbing off the top of the bank. Sherrill stayed in the saddle, using his heels to urge the stallion forward.

Some of the wounded groaned and screamed. Others writhed in silence. A few breathed raggedly in their unconsciousness.

A moment after the barrage of rifle fire had ended, the noise in the church was curtailed. But anguish was vented again as a new volley of shots exploded.

Grinning in keen enjoyment of their task, the eight

14

men emptied their rifles into the defenseless forms of the wounded. And, when hammers clicked against vacant breeches, they drew revolvers and blasted the last sign of life from the survivors.

Silver-miners, storekeepers, clerks, a schoolteacher, the undertaker . . . Sherrill knew them all. And blamed them all. Would have wished to see them all die the same brand of agonized death he had inflicted upon the judge. But that had not been possible. There were too many of them and he did not have the men nor the time to slake his thirst for vengeance so thoroughly.

But, as he surveyed the result of the massacre—the twisted limbs, the blood-soaked clothing, the contorted faces—he nodded and expressed a degree of satisfaction. It had been like it once was in Kansas and Missouri. He had realized his own and the limitation of the force under his command. He had planned accordingly and achieved the extent of the success that was possible.

There was an explosion behind him and he was once more jerked out of mental reverie. His self-anger lasted longer this time. Perhaps for a full two seconds, but, when he turned his stallion, no trace of it showed on his face.

The horses and burro had been brought back down Main Street from the saloon. Five of the men were already mounted. Smoke was billowing from the open door and shattered windows of the bank. The mutilated corpse was still swinging to and fro in the after effects of the blast.

The other mounted men waited as patiently as he did. For all of three minutes. Then Bergen and the bald-headed, round-shouldered John Slade emerged from the bank, clear of smoke now. They carried several bulging saddlebags, which were slung across the back of the burro and lashed securely in place. As the two men swung up into their saddles, Thad Bergen pushed his fingers into his mouth and sounded a shrill whistle.

15

All was still inside the church now. Running footfalls sounded from the back of it. Then hoofbeats as Mitchell and Gomez rode their horses across the graveyard and out onto the body-littered street.

It had taken two days to ride deep into Sonora and find the hacienda where Judge King was staying with a Mexican friend. And another two days to ride north to Borderville. During both legs of the long journey, Clyde Sherrill had taken the lead of an orderly column, eight men riding two abreast with Wheeler Mitchell bringing up the rear and leading the burro.

The same formation was adopted now, for the ride along Main Street and out onto the open trail.

"Them females and kids still ain't come outta the church," Mitchell reported flatly after glancing back with his one eye as he led the burro beyond the town marker.

"Guess they know what's waitin' outside," Thad Bergen rasped as he ejected the final spent shellcase from his Frontier Colt and started to feed fresh rounds into the chambers. "And ain't anxious to see it."

He grinned at the thoughtful Manuel Gomez who was riding beside him just ahead of Mitchell.

"*Si*," the Mexican responded absently.

"Hey, what's wrong with you?" the youngster wanted to know.

Gomez shrugged. "In the old days, it was better. After the killing, *muchacho*, there were always the women. In the church was *la bella señorita*. With the hair like ripened wheat and such a body."

He put the tips of a thumb and forefinger to his lips and kissed them noisily.

"Shame on you, *hombre*!" the one-eyed Mitchell chided cheerfully. "And you only two weeks away from being married."

The Mexican's expression was mock serious as he looked over his shoulder.

16

"Just because a man has ordered a fat and lazy burro . . ." a broad grin split his dark-skinned features, ". . . it does not mean he cannot wish to possess a wild and beautiful mare."

CHAPTER TWO

When the sun was clear of the eastern ridges the next morning, and strong enough to burn off the final traces of the night's cold, Adam Steele removed his sheepskin coat and pushed it under the strap which held his bedroll in place behind his saddle. A half hour later he took off his gray suit jacket and stowed it in the same way.

His once-white shirt was already stained with the sweat of the new day and he continued to perspire freely as he rode the piebald gelding slowly south on the little-used trail through the hills.

It was an ornate shirt, with ruffled collar and pearl buttons worn under a green velvet vest. The jacket he had just shed and the matching pants were of fine material, finely tailored. His boots, which he wore inside the pants cuffs, were plainly styled but of the best quality. Likewise his black hat.

But every item of apparel had seen better days and had served the man well. Oldest of all—and showing the most signs of hard wear and long travel—was a gray silk kerchief with two weighted corners which hung loosely about his neck, and the sheepskin coat.

A slit in the outside seam of his right pants leg—between ankle and knee—had not been caused by hard wear.

The owner of the clothing was a little older than thirty years and had a compact build reaching to a height of about five feet six inches. His face had lean lines, the sparse flesh darkened and cracked by extremes of weather. The features were regular, with a certain hardness in the coal-black eyes counterbalanced by a quality of gentleness in the line of his mouth. He was clean-shaven and the neatly trimmed hair that showed at his sideburns and beneath the brim of his hat was gray, streaked frugally with strands of red.

It was a face that possessed a brand of nondescript handsomeness, lacking character in repose.

There was no gunbelt at his waist, but the stock and frame of a Colt Hartford revolving rifle jutted from the boot hung forward on the right side of his saddle. The rosewood of the stock was scarred by burning and a small, gold plate was screwed to one side of it. The split in his pants leg allowed him access to a wooden-handled knife resting in a boot sheath. Equally deadly as the rifle and knife was the silk scarf he wore as a kerchief.

But it was almost two months ago, in the Great Basin of Nevada, when he had last had occasion to use his skills in the art of killing. Since then, he had spent some quiet days at Fort Remington and many more even quieter days on the long journey south.

He was in southern Arizona Territory now, having crossed the Gila River Trail west of Tucson, heading for Mexico. There had been settlements on his route—a town here and there, a farm-stead, a ranch, an army fort, an Indian village. And fellow human beings on the move, in pairs or larger groups. But if trouble had ever been close, it had never threatened Steele.

Nevertheless, he maintained a careful watch on his surroundings as he rode the barren country, intent upon seeing potential danger the moment it showed. It was his way because it had often been the reason he survived—and survival had become the sole reason for his existence.

It was an hour after he took off his suit jacket that he saw the group of men riding up the trail toward him. The trail from the north had curved around a high bluff to enter a broad valley. As Steele rode into one end, the men entered the other, about a mile away. A heat shimmer had just begun to develop and the group of horsemen were seen as a distorted image at first. They were riding at the same easy pace as Steele and it was a full five minutes before he got a clear impression of them.

The valley floor sloped gently down in a southward direction so that, from the higher elevation, Steele was able to count ten riders. Eight of them riding double file, one at the head and another bringing up the rear, with a burro on a lead line. At first he thought the men comprised an army patrol for there was a military aspect to the column. But, as the gap narrowed, he saw that they did not wear uniforms.

He watched them carefully from behind a façade of nonchalance, and sensed that he was the object of a similar scrutiny. When a hundred feet separated the group from him, the gaunt-faced man at the head of the column raised a hand and every horse was reined to a halt.

"Morning to you!" Clyde Sherrill greeted without warmth, Texas in his accent.

"How are you?" Steele responded, halting his gelding ten feet in front of Sherrill. His own voice had a drawl that told of the Virginian background. He smiled and the expression took better than five years off his age.

None of the men responsible for the massacre at Borderville matched Steele's expression. They all continued to eye him coldly, suspiciously. They were unshaven for several days and dirty. Dust clung to their clothing and their horses. All were armed with Winchester rifles and wore gunbelts.

"Business in Borderville?" Sherrill asked.

"Borderville?"

The gaunt-faced man jerked a thumb over his shoulder. "Trail ends at Borderville. Get there by nightfall at the rate you've been riding. Mexico beyond that. A long way to anywhere."

"Grateful for the information," the Virginian drawled. "Get some supplies in Borderville?"

A nod. "That won't be any problem. You're not looking for work?"

"Mostly I am. If it appeals to me."

Another nod from Sherrill, with a tightening of the mouthline. "There could be work for you at Borderville. Of the kind that might appeal to a man like you. But you consider the offer very carefully, mister."

Sherrill was no longer looking at Steele. He had made his survey of the quiet-spoken Virginian and reached his conclusion. Steele looked like a dude drummer fallen on hard times and he didn't wear a gunbelt. But Sherrill discounted appearances and detected a latent menace behind the outer shell of the man.

"That all?" Steele asked, dropping the smile and pursing his lips reflectively. The change of expression emphasized the hardness in his dark eyes.

"Just some advice, mister. Take it or ignore it. My men and I are happy to let bygones be bygones. We aren't looking for trouble."

"But we're ready to handle it if it happens," Matt Webb said from behind Sherrill. He was about forty, broad at the shoulders and thick at the waist. Bristles did not grow on old scar tissues at his right cheek.

"And we're old hands at it," the man beside him added. He was Vincent Bowton. A rangy thirty-five year old with red hair and green eyes. He had one stirrup lower than the other, as if his left leg was permanently stiff.

It was Steele's turn to nod. "We're riding in different directions, but we've got a lot in common."

"That's what I figured," Sherrill responded, looking

21

satisfied. "Nice talking to you, mister. Guess we won't run into each other again?"

He raised his eyebrows to add the query, but did not wait for an answer. His right hand was extended into the air and pushed forward. Then he tugged gently on the reins to steer his big stallion into a curve round Steele. The men behind him responded to the tacit order and followed his course, riding clear of where the Virginian remained stationary in the center of the trail. Silent suspicion was directed at him from several pairs of eyes. A few of the men expressed a silent warning.

Nobody looked back at him after the burro with the bulging saddlebags had been led past him. The pace was as slow as it had been before, with only small puffs of dust being raised by the clopping hooves.

But Steele watched them, turning in the saddle. Mildly irritated by the thinly veiled threat, he did not entirely trust the implication that it was meant to dissuade him from future action. So he watched the slow-moving column until it became distorted by heat shimmer and then moved out of sight around the bluff.

He touched his heels to the gelding's flanks then clicked his tongue against the roof of his mouth. The horse started south once more, plodding over the sign left by the group. The rider resumed his three-hundred-and-sixty-degree watch on the country. And saw nothing except a cloudless sky and inhospitable land: a blistering panorama against which nothing moved except himself, his horse and the broiling sun. He experienced no sense of being watched.

In the early afternoon he reached the end of the hill country and made camp on the edge of the scrub desert. Others had made camp here recently and he guessed the ten men had spent the night beside the tiny water hole with its surrounding patch of grass and semicircle of mixed greasewood and mesquite. There was enough forage left for the gelding. Steele ate sparingly from his almost exhausted supplies, unsure whether to trust the information about Borderville.

Then he resumed his ride south. His searching eyes saw no more white men—American or Mexican. No Apaches. No military patrols. No sign of human or animal life until he rounded a sandstone bluff and peered along the final stretch of trail at the small town of Borderville.

The sun was still clear of the western ridges and had not yet begun to change color from yellow to crimson. The heat was still high.

The first movement to catch Steele's watchful eyes was at the top of the church tower. A bell clanged once, indicating what had moved. Then again and again, in the slow cadence of a death knell.

Steele's gelding pricked its ears, but continued to move forward, matching its pace to the tuneless toll of the bell. Closer, level with the town marker—BORDERVILLE: ELEVATION 150 FEET: POPULATION 201—the animal balked. But Steele spoke softly to him and stroked his neck. Then caught the scent which had disturbed the horse. It was an odor with which the Virginian had become familiar during the War between the States and had smelt often since then: the over-ripe, sickly sweet stench of dead flesh left unburied.

There were houses at the north end of Main Street. They flanked it for half its length. The business premises—a saloon, several stores, a livery stable, a newspaper office, the sheriff's office, the Borderville Bank. The smell of the unburied dead grew stronger in the warm air of late afternoon as he neared the meeting point of the two streets. The bell continued to toll in the mournful frequency of death.

He halted the gelding in the middle of the street at the side of the bank and the animal felt tense beneath him. He saw the blasted door and shattered windows of the bank, the many brown patches of dried

23

blood in front of the church and the countless ejected shellcases lying all around. He made his survey through apparently disinterested eyes but, behind the impassive expression, his mind was working with calm concentration, building a black and white picture of what had happened in this town. The coloring of detail might be provided later—if he considered it important to his own well-being.

The smell of decomposing flesh was very strong now, emanating from beyond the bank on Mine Road, held like a palpable presence among the buildings which appeared to be deserted. The sense that he was being watched had also increased in strength as he moved deeper into the center of town.

After looking at the obvious signs of old trouble, he concentrated on the church. Not because it was from here that the bell tolled; for more insistent in his mind than the monotonous note of the single-tone dirge was the conviction that eyes were peering out at him from the church.

"Make a sudden move, mister—and we'll be ringing it for you as well."

The Virginian vented a low grunt of satisfaction that his sense of the proximity of watching eyes had been proved correct again. He raked his own gaze along the four slit windows which faced the street and then fixed it on the porch as he draped one hand over his saddlehorn and touched the brim of his hat with the other. "I won't tempt providence, ma'am."

Abruptly, the knell ceased to sound. Silence swooped in from the surrounding country and pressed an oppressive weight over the town. The sun turned red and the air felt hotter. The scent of death smelled stronger.

"What?" the same woman demanded from just inside the porch of the church.

"Won't ask for whom the bell tolls."

"Who are you and what do you want here?"

24

She stepped across the porch and out on to the open street. A handsome woman in her late thirties with a slender figure and blonde hair held in a tight bun. She was dressed in a white Sunday-best gown, stained by dirt and dried blood. She was holding an old .54 Symmes rifle, breechloading percussion, single shot. She aimed it unsteadily at Steele from her shoulder. A half dozen other women crowded into the porch behind her. They were unarmed. Like their spokeswoman, they had also been doing some unpleasant work in their best dresses.

"Looking for a place to rest up the night and buy some supplies for when I move on tomorrow," the Virginian replied evenly.

His awareness of watching eyes was a facet of the sixth sense that had been born in war and developed during the years of the violent peace. This was allied to the constant and involuntary alertness of the man. He was still confident that all the anxious interest in his arrival was coming from the church. But the women he could see and those who remained hidden witnessed no sign of complacency about him. Although his tone was even and polite, there was a visible harshness in his face.

"Be grateful if you'd get on with your business and allow me to go about mine," he urged.

"He ain't one of 'em, Margery!" a woman in the porch said shrilly.

She was fat and fifty, with a deeply lined face that was dark with a Latin ancestry. Her hair was jet black, long and unkempt. As she spoke, more women stepped out into the porch. Others showed their faces at the slit windows.

Steele surveyed them all briefly and could see that each was under attack by a variety of strong emotions: grief, anger or fear. And he knew he was the instigator of the last.

25

"Claire's right!" a woman inside the church urged. "Let's do what we have to."

Margery Salisbury, the widow of the town's druggist, continued to train the ancient rifle on Steele for a further two seconds. Then she unclenched her fists from around the frame and barrel and the Symmes clattered to the stone floor of the porch.

"All right, stranger," she rasped. "But don't you go making free with anything in this town. It's all closed up until after the cremation."

"You want me to pay in advance for stabling my horse?" Steele asked.

The overweight Claire shook her head as the rest of the women made to go back into the church. "Livery's mine now Frank's gone. Bed your animal down and I'll be along presently."

The Virginian tipped his hat to her and wheeled the gelding as the woman went into the church. Then he dismounted and led the horse toward the livery stable, which was directly across the street from the Far West Saloon. Behind him, feet shuffled on the floor of the church. A few moments later the pump-organ started to whine out the opening chords of a hymn. Then massed voices—of women and children—launched into a strangely beautiful rendition of the Twenty-Third Psalm.

Ten of the twelve stalls in the stable were occupied. The horses, familiar with the odor of rotting flesh, were calm. By the time Steele had unsaddled his gelding, watered him and used a pitchfork to tip a bale of hay down from the loft, his mount was as docile as the other animals in the livery stable. Then the Virginian put feed in the trough, secured the stall and stepped out through the rear door.

All the time, the melodious and melancholy hymn singing continued to drift along the town's two streets from the church. Then, as he climbed up on to a wheel-

26

less wagon and lowered himself onto the seat, the singing ended. The bell began to toll once more. He had brought a half-full canteen outside with him and he sipped at the tepid contents, washing the trail dust from his throat and enjoying the luxury of knowing that there was plenty of water close by.

He looked from the rear of the livery stable toward the backs of the buildings lining the east side of Mine Road. Behind one of them, which was across the street from the two-story courthouse, a glass-sided hearse was parked. At first, it did not seem to be a building at all—rather, a neatly stacked pile of hay bales. But he glimpsed the white of an adobe wall between some of the bales.

The source of the odor of rotting flesh emanated from inside the walls and hay bales. Mixed with it was the pungent smell of kerosene with which the hay had been doused.

The bell continued to clang.

Three women appeared at the rear of the doomed building. As they glanced across at him, he saw their eyes were red-rimmed and that the sinking sun glinted on fresh tears tracking down their grimed cheeks.

Each took a kitchen match from a box held by one of them, struck it, waited for the death knell to end, then set fire to the kerosene-soaked hay.

They moved quickly then, running down the alley between the funeral parlor and a store.

The pyre blazed, flames leaping and a pall of black smoke swirling high into the warm air above Borderville. Louder than the crackle of flames was the wailing and shrieking of women and children who watched the cremation from Mine Road.

Soon, smudges of soot began to fall, marking the white adobe of surrounding buildings. Then sparks rose from the crackling flames, drifted, hovered and touched down. While the women vented their anguish, detached

27

from everything beyond their grief, children scuttled to and fro with water pails and flails to douse the many small fires before they took hold.

There was a loud crack and the roof and two walls of the funeral parlor collapsed. The smoke was thicker for a few moments, then became wispy amid the raging flames. Steele was able to see across the fire then, at the three rows of weeping women aligned in front of the courthouse. Their grief was less vocal and the sounds of the fire masked their sobs.

The evil smell of over-roasted human meat permeated the town. Or perhaps a man who did not know what meat was cooking would find the smell appetizing.

There were no more sparks and the breathless young firefighters hurried to join their mothers, some urging them to leave the pyre.

Steele climbed down from the wagon and went through the livery stable and out onto Main Street. The horses had been perturbed when they first smelled smoke. But they were calm again now. The sun was three-quarters hidden behind the ridges in the west. Low in the east the sky was already dark.

He crossed to the sidewalk in front of the saloon. As he stepped up on to the boarding, several women and children rounded the angle of the bank and started up Main. All of them had emerged from the full depth of their misery.

"Can I get dinner and a room for the night here?" Steele called.

Claire Johnston, widow of the livery stable owner, detached herself from the group and went into the stable. Another woman angled toward where Steele waited outside the swing doors of the saloon. The remainder continued on down toward the houses at the north end of the street.

"Room and eatin' both, mister. But food'll be cold. I'm not up to cookin' today."

The woman who brushed past Steele and went through the doorway was about forty. She was a thin redhead with a careworn face and stooped shoulders. The lines of bitterness inscribed in her skin had been cut long before the events which led to the mass cremation.

He followed her inside. The room was square, with the bar running down one side and a stairway canting across the rear wall. There was a grand piano on a platform against the wall opposite the bar. Under the slope of the stairway were two pool tables. Most of the central floor space was taken up by chair-ringed tables. There was a stove at either side of the platform.

The saloon was filled with the darkness and chill of evening, and the distant odors of much drinking and smoking and eating. It was scarred from use but clean.

"They came while we were at Sunday evenin' service," the woman said dully as she moved from one end of the bar to the other, lighting two kerosene lamps. "On Sundays, we never open for business until after the evenin' service. Beer or hard liquor?"

Steele had advanced to the bar and it was a moment before he realized the woman had stopped talking about Sunday and was asking him what he wanted to drink.

"I gave up alcohol a long time ago," he replied. "Coffee while you're fixing the meal?"

"Seein' as the food'll be cold, be ready at about the same time."

She moved down to the far end of the bar and through an open doorway in the rear wall. Steele sat down at the nearest table as a deeper darkness and chiller cold crept in over and under the swing doors. The two lamps attacked the night but the stoves were unlit. The woman made no sound out in the kitchen.

After a while, Steele stood up and left the saloon. There was just a faint red and yellow glow from the dying fire in the funeral parlor and the smell of the

29

charred bodies was hardly detectable. Main Street was deserted. There were lights in the windows of the houses at the north end and smoke curled up from their chimneys. The half moon was beginning to glitter.

As Steele entered the livery stable from the front, the widow of its former owner turned away from the rear doorway, from where she had been watching the fire burn across the way.

"You're not leavin'?" she asked anxiously.

"It's getting cold," he replied as he went to where he had left his saddle and bedroll outside the gelding's stall. "I guess the lady who runs the saloon has had enough of fires for one day."

He worked his jacket and coat loose from the bedroll and put them on. Claire Johnston nodded and turned her back to him again.

"Or maybe Amy Richards is just too bone-deep weary to light the stoves, mister. Ain't none of us had a wink of sleep since Sunday mornin'. And that seems like a lifetime ago. They killed every one of our menfolk. You got to excuse the way the town is right now."

As Steele turned to leave, he saw the stock of his rifle jutting from the boot. He did a double take at it, then peered into the palms of his empty hands. Anger flared into his dark eyes for a moment, then he jerked the rifle from the boot and canted it to his shoulder before leaving the livery stable. The woman was still watching the fire, her fleshy back trembling with silent sobs.

Smoke was wisping from one of the saloon's chimneys as he crossed the empty street. He smelled coffee as he re-entered the building, but had been seated at the table for more than five minutes before Amy Richards came out with a tray bearing a plate of cold beef and potatoes and a mug of coffee.

"We used to be able to do a lot better," she said as she delivered his order, then started to go behind the

30

bar. "Maybe we'll get back to the old ways again . . . some time."

"Grateful for this much, ma'am," Steele told her, taking off his hat and hooking it over the muzzle of the Colt Hartford, the rifle leaning against the edge of the table.

He ate in silence for several minutes, enjoying the fresh food and the coffee which was strong with newly ground beans.

"Don't you want to know what happened?" the woman asked at length. She had appeared to be locked in a private world of undemonstrative grief and unaware of him.

"Does it concern me, ma'am?" Steele countered.

She rubbed fists in her red-rimmed eyes, to clear them of the grit of fatigue rather than dried tears. "Such wanton, cold-blooded slaughter should be the concern of every decent human being." Her emotional reserves were too low to give force to the taunt.

"Some would say that lets me out," the Virginian told her.

The church bell clanged. Just once. Steele was startled for an instant, the single note sounding much louder in the dark of night than when he had heard the start of the death knell earlier.

"I have to go," Amy Richards announced dully. "The meetin's about to start."

There was a vagueness in her voice. And her movements as she came out from behind the bar, weaved between the tables and pushed through the swing doors had a jerky, almost mechanical quality about them. Although he could not see them, Steele heard other women on the street and sidewalks. But the town was in a clamp of silence again by the time he finished the meal.

It was difficult to pinpoint precisely when he had ceased to be a decent human being. It had not been

31

before the war when, as the son of one of the richest plantation owners in Virginia, he had used his wealth and privilege wisely. In the early months of the war, fighting for the Confederacy, he had attempted to control his personal bitterness; to meet the enemy in battle with honor, detached from the awareness that his father had elected to support the Union. And he had succeeded.

It was the harshness and horror of war itself which had forced him to abandon the abstracts of honor and causes. When, like every other man on both sides, he discovered the grim reality that, if his life was the prize, he would resort to any means to win it.

Thus, as the war made its ravaging progress through time and across terrain, Adam Steele committed countless crimes which, in a time of peace, would be considered inhuman. The animosity he felt toward his father augmented his will to survive and his uniform provided the excuse which exonerated him from guilt.

The war ended and his father made an overture toward repairing the split in the Steele family. And, no longer in the uniform of a cavalry lieutenant constantly in danger of being blasted or cut to pieces by a Union attack, the son was willing to accept.

Adam Steele went to Washington, prepared to forget the immediate past, recall the years before the war and to rebuild what had once been. Perhaps it could never have happened; perhaps the euphoria of peace which the elder and the younger Steele experienced veiled the old bitterness rather than extinguished it. There was no chance to find out. For the war was not over for others.

And, on the night Abraham Lincoln was assassinated, Ben Steele was lynched from a beam in a barroom, across Tenth Street from Ford's Theatre.

Adam Steele found him there, cut him down and shot a man; for a personal cause and with no uniform to excuse the act.

Perhaps it was when he saw his father's body hanging by the neck in a stinking barroom that Adam Steele became less than human. Or when he shot the man. Certainly the violent peace began then.

He took the body of his father back to Virginia and found the plantation and house in charred ruins. He buried Ben Steele in the family plot, then followed a trail halfway across the continent to kill every man responsible for the lynching.

This personal war lasted only a fraction of the time it had taken the Union to subdue the Confederacy. And there was no euphoria when it was over. Not even the sweet taste of revenge. For he was wanted on a charge of murder and the lawman who tracked him down was his best friend.

Adam Steele killed Deputy Jim Bishop. Showing him no more mercy, perhaps, than the men who had ridden into Borderville and massacred every man in the town.

"We have a proposition for you, mister."

Again, the Virginian was startled by a sound that ended the long, hard, melancholy silence. His chair was sideways onto the saloon entrance and he turned just his head to look toward the swing doors.

Margery Salisbury stepped across the threshold. Instead of the Symmes, she was holding a worn carpetbag. Amy Richards was behind her on the left and Claire Johnston on the right. The handsome blonde woman moved deeper into the saloon and the other two stayed at the entrance, holding the doors open. Through the doorway Steele could see the rest of the women, standing in a tight, silent group. Grief was still plain to see on every face. But there was also grim determination visible in the eyes and set of the mouthlines.

The widow of Borderville's druggist halted across the table from Steele, but made no attempt to sit down. She held the bag in two hands and rested it on the back of a chair.

33

"Six months ago, a man named Clyde Sherrill was tried for murder in the town courthouse. He was found guilty." Mrs Salisbury had bathed and changed into a mourning dress since Steele had last seen her. The pallor of her face was emphasized by the black she wore. In the lamplight her features looked even more handsome. Her brown eyes were fixed upon infinity an inch above the Virginian's head. "He was a local citizen," she continued in the same dispassionate tone. "Worked out at the silver mine and provided a house in town for his wife and baby. Nice folks, seemed like."

"They went north, ma'am," Steele said. "I'm heading south."

Mrs. Salisbury nodded, looked at him briefly, then leaned forward and up-ended the carpetbag over the table. Jewelry spilled out, along with bills and coins. Bracelets, necklaces, earrings, brooches, rings, hatpins. Mostly silver, but some gold. A few plain pieces, but most set with precious stones. The bills seemed to be mainly ones, fives and tens. Coins of every denomination. Some money and items of jewelry bounced off the table and onto the floor.

The woman straightened up and hung the bag over the back of the chair. She fixed her gaze on the point above Steele's head again, without watching him for a reaction.

"Clyde Sherrill held up our bank. He just walked in, drew a gun and demanded money. He was given what he asked for. And he almost escaped with it. But some children were playin' out on Main Street. The folks in the bank yelled about the robbery. Sherrill raced his horse, and ran down two children of three and four years old. Broke open their skulls. Sherrill was stunned and brought his horse down. Didn't know where he was until he'd been in Sheriff Brown's jailhouse for two days."

Steele continued to listen, but no longer looked at the

woman. Instead, he started to pick out the bills from the littered table top, stacking and counting them.

"Trial was the next day. Jury found him guilty in ten minutes and Judge King said he was to hang. But Mrs. Sherrill, she got someone from the Territorial Governor's office to say the trial wasn't fair. On account of bias. Feller said there'd have to be a new trial—in Tucson. Sure we were biased. Everyone in town knew the children that were killed and knew their parents. But more than thirty people saw Sherrill rob the bank and gallop over the children!"

She glared directly into Steele's impassive face now, as if challenging him to fault her. He had finished stacking and counting the bills. They added up to two hundred and thirty-one dollars.

"Sherrill escaped?" the Virginian asked. "Or was acquitted?"

The intensity faded from the woman's eyes. "The men attempted to take him from the jailhouse and string him up. Only Sheriff Brown prevented it. His sister's child was one of those Sherrill killed. Mr. Brown said the men would have to kill him to get to Sherrill." She nodded her head. "Even now, after what happened yesterday, we're grateful to the sheriff for his stand. Even though, on the way to Tucson, Sherrill escaped from the Territorial Marshals. At least our menfolk died without the sin of lynchin' weighin' on their conscience."

"How about your consciences, ladies?" Steele asked levelly, shifting his dark eyes from Mrs. Salisbury to the women in the doorway and back again. "No sin to pay a man two hundred and thirty-one dollars to do your killing for you?"

"The jewelry will fetch better than two thousand, we figure," Mrs. Salisbury rasped. "And we'll do our own dirty dishes, mister. Just need you to gather them up for us." She waved a hand over the table. "This is for expenses while you hunt them down. Everythin' of value

35

we have left. Sherrill and his thugs emptied the bank. You can keep every cent they ain't spent. All you got to do is bring them back to Borderville. Ten of them. Sherrill's a tall, thin-faced feller with—"

"Know what he looks like," Steele cut in, and the interruption produced a gasp from the women in the doorway and spread a frown across the face of Margery Salisbury. "And the nine men riding with him."

"How? Who are you? What—?"

"Name's Steele. Met them on the trail this morning. Warned me to think deep about any job I might be offered in this town."

Amy Richards made a sound that was akin to the start of a hysterical laugh. Then she whirled and rushed out on to the street. The women gathered around her as she began to report the item of news.

"Then that makes it far easier!" the widow of the druggist exclaimed, excitement showing through the darker emotions in her eyes. "If you've seen them and will recognize them again, you have only—"

"I have only two hundred and thirty-one dollars. And no guarantee of finding the money with the men. I'm not in the used trinket business."

Now the woman expressed contempt, but managed to veil it an instant after Steele had seen it. "There was at least thirty thousand in the bank safe. If you are man enough to find the murderers, surely you can find the money they stole?"

"Tell him about Julia, Margery," Claire Johnston urged from the doorway, then looked over her shoulder and shouted, "Julia!"

There was movement in the crowd of women and one of them emerged from the press and advanced across the street. She stepped up on to the sidewalk and pushed open the swing doors to stand in the place vacated by the widow of the saloon owner. She was eighteen or nineteen with a fine body just reached maturity. Her

36

pretty face was fresh with the bloom of youth, her eyes pale green and her sun-bronzed skin unblemished. She had brown hair that tumbled over her shoulders and down her back in long, thick waves. Even the look of terror on her face did not mar her beauty.

"This is Julia King, Mr. Steele," Margery Salisbury said, a croak in her tone. "The orphaned granddaughter of the judge whom Sherrill and his thugs tortured and dragged naked into Borderville last night. She is a . . ." The new widow's pallor was abruptly driven from her face by a blush of deep crimson. She closed her eyes tight to speak one word. ". . . virgin. She has volunteered to give herself to you until such time as you tire of her."

The young girl trembled, then became rock still, fists clenched and big eyes staring sightlessly in front of her. Steele glanced briefly at her then concentrated on Mrs. Salisbury again.

"Of course," the woman went on, still flushed by shame and embarrassment, "should there be another woman more to your taste, other arrangements can be made."

Ever since the young girl had been summoned forward and he had guessed what kind of offer was being made to him, Steele had been struggling to quell a rising anger that threatened to erupt. Now, as Mrs. Salisbury waited anxiously for his response, he succeeded. And the fact that the woman expressed only concern showed she had not seen through his dispassionate façade.

"Go to hell, lady," he said softly.

Mrs. Salisbury gasped. "You won't help us?"

Steele ran the backs of his fingers along the bristles on his jawline. "Sure I'll help. Which is the reason you'll go to hell. Along with anyone else in this town who intends to make Sherrill and his bunch pay without resort to the law."

"That is our concern. And I assure you, sir, we will

be grateful to you in this instance as we were to Sheriff Brown when he prevented the earlier evil."

The Virginian stood up, put on his hat, then lifted the rifle with one hand and the stack of bills with the other. "He get the pick of the local beauties, ma'am?"

Shamefaced, the woman shook her head. "No, of course not. Nor money, neither. Mr. Brown was simply doin' the job he was paid for."

"Same as I intend to," Steele replied as he started across the saloon toward the foot of the stairway. "After a night's rest."

He moved up the creaking treads.

"You don't wish . . . for company?" Mrs. Salisbury called.

Julia King was looking at Steele now, her lips parted after she had sucked in a deep breath and held it, her eyes wide with anxious hope. Steele touched the brim of his hat toward the young girl and the two women who had crowded up onto the sidewalk when he agreed to take the job.

"No offense intended for any of you ladies," he said and smiled bleakly. "But I reckon a town in mourning is no place for a ball."

CHAPTER THREE

Steele awoke in the cold darkness of an hour before dawn. He had slept soundly, confident of his sense for danger which would rouse him if he was threatened. During the night, slight noises in the quiet town caused him to rise close to the surface of awareness, but always he sank back again to the shallow level of restful sleep.

There was total silence throughout Borderville as he went down into the saloon and discovered the reason for some of the sounds which had disturbed him briefly during the night. One of the stoves had been lit, but not for the comfort of warmth in the pre-dawn chill. On a nearby table there was a pot of water, a basin, a razor, some towels and a bar of soap. On another was a bowl, a mug, a jug of coffee grounds already in it, and the makings of a bacon, egg, potato and beans breakfast in a skillet.

He lit a lamp and took advantage of all the preparations, then went out into the cold start of the new day and across to the livery stable. He was conscious of eyes watching him from the second floor of the saloon.

There were only six horses in the stalls now, including his own piebald gelding. The canteens and bags hung on his saddle were heavy with the essential needs of a man riding in open country.

He mounted inside the stable and rode the horse out, maintaining an easy walking pace after he had turned to head north along Main Street. Eyes continued to watch him from the Far West Saloon, then he became aware of scrutiny from closer quarters as he rode between the houses. The hooves of the gelding left new signs in the dust of the street. There was a heavy dew on the ground, so that Steele was able to see that the horses taken from the livery stable earlier had also been ridden north.

A young child cried out in the darkness, perhaps frightened by a nightmare. Steele had ridden clear of the town by then and the cry was the only sound in Borderville. After it, the town again became as silent as it was dark.

Expelled breath from the nostrils of the gelding and the mouth of the man showed as gray vapor. It came thicker and faster when the Virginian demanded a gallop on the open trail. When he felt warm inside his coat and the coat of the gelding showed the first lather of sweat, he reined back to an easy canter. Later, he eased the pace down to a walk again. And pulled a pair of gloves from his top coat pocket.

The gloves were a relic of war. Of scuffed and stained black buckskin they comprised a kind of good luck charm for a man who did not believe in luck. Perhaps at first, during some war-torn, bitter-cold winter back east, he had worn the gloves as protection against the weather. Or, maybe, from some deep-seated desire to keep blood off his hands. He could not remember. Latterly though, his conscious thought as he drew on the gloves was always concerned with impending trouble. And, in meeting the most dangerous kind of trouble, he considered the wearing of the gloves as important as his deadly skill with the Colt Hartford and the knife.

He rode through the morning, halted for a while at midday and then, by turns, rode and led the piebald gelding. There was no need to follow the sign left by Sherrill and his men until he was through the valley where he had met them a day and a half ago. But he did check the trail ahead occasionally to make sure the women who had left Borderville were still moving in the same direction.

The killers—and some of the women they had made widows—had swung to the west three miles north of the low-sided valley. It was an hour before sundown when the Virginian veered off the main trail and started along a narrow canyon. At the far end, where the ground rose steeply and only a well-trodden, zig-zag pathway kept the canyon from being a blind one, he found the spot where the Sherrill bunch had made night camp. There were the charred remains of a fire, cigarette and cigar butts, scraps of discarded food and heaps of horse droppings. There was no sign to indicate that the women had halted here and Steele himself paused only briefly. Then he had to lead his nervous gelding up the narrow, hairpinned pathway.

At the top the rocky ground sloped gently away to the southwest, the hillside pocked with the tunnel openings of ancient silver mines. The fallen, rotted and sunbleached timbers of many abandoned shacks were also scattered across the slope. There was no layer of dust on the exposed ground and no clearly defined trail leading away from the old claims—except the pathway down into the canyon.

As the sun sank and changed color, Steele allowed his horse to rest while he swung to and fro in a series of lengthening semicircles; from south, out to the west and back toward the north. The horse droppings he found indicated a due-west direction. The sign was at least a day old.

He washed up and shaved, lit a fire and made coffee and a meal. Then, feeling the effects of the long day's travel less badly, he led his horse westward through a night that became colder as it brightened with moon and starlight.

41

There was another halt two hours later, at a patch of scrub grass in a cottonwood grove. After the gelding had eaten—where no other horse had fed for much longer than two days—he watered him and climbed into the saddle.

Steele had seen no more signs after the horse droppings at the mine workings and he did no more tracking. Instead, he rode as directly as the terrain allowed toward a cluster of gleaming lights. They were southwest from the cottonwoods, on higher ground and at least five miles distant.

The intervening ground was in the form of a series of rocky valleys, cutting north to south as if some prehistoric giant had clawed a massive hand to tear in a fit of savage anger at the once flat landscape.

Close to the hill from which the lights gleamed, Steele lost sight of them as the incline was steep. He climbed it, once more leading the gelding, and did not see the lights again until he reached the crest. Where the rise finished, the land flattened abruptly, to form a broad plateau. Featured only with cactus and strewn boulders on this side. Beyond, was a town. Of sorts.

It was bathed in bright moonlight and the gleam from countless lamps. As Steele rode closer he could see the various stages of the community's development—clearly defined by the styles of architecture and materials used.

It had started out as a simple Mexican mission. Then a Mexican army post had been established. Later a few crude houses had been built outside the walls of the fort. The church, fort and houses still showed battle scars of bullet holes and burning. The United States army had taken control, repairing the fort's crumbled adobe with timber. But the repair work had rotted and fallen.

Since the military had left, there had been a great deal of construction, in adobe, stone and timber. All of it hurried and ugly with no thought to town planning.

42

The mission, fort and original houses were on the north side, built around three sides of a plaza. The rest of the town straggled southward for close to half a mile in a series of short streets, never more than three or four buildings long. The first row faced onto the plaza with the fort across the way. All the others looked out at the back lots of the buildings in front of them. Narrow alleys cut between buildings.

Almost every one of the new buildings was devoted to the pleasures of entertainment or eating. And business was booming. There were saloons, dancehalls, cantinas, theatres, restaurants, bordellos and a dozen different kinds of carnival sideshows.

Music, laughter and raised voices competed to make the most strident noise. The result was a bedlam of sound that seemed to give movement to the bitter cold air of a night in which not the faintest breeze stirred.

Steele rode on to the plaza through the huddle of old Mexican houses and saw that they were all as deserted and derelict as the fort and the church.

"Welcome to Carly, stranger!" a woman yelled. "You've hit the right end of town. We've got the best action at the cheapest prices."

She stood in the doorway of the center building of the three facing the plaza. Like every other building in town, it was single-story. Along the roof was a garishly painted sign proclaiming: HOUSE OF PLEASURE. On one side of the cat house there was the timber-built Arizona Saloon and on the other side the adobe Sonora Cantina.

Light gleamed at the windows of all three buildings. The drinking places were noisy with the music of pianos, fiddles and guitars against a counterpoint of talk and laughter. The only sound from the House of Pleasure was the voice of the enormously fat woman wrapped in a massive fur coat who grinned broadly at Steele and beckoned frantically to him.

43

"Take your pick, stranger! All the colors of the rainbow and all the tricks of the world!"

Her laughter was uglier than her voice and her face. So that the wares on display in the four brightly lit windows at the front of the building probably gained by comparison. There was a Negress, an Apache girl, a Chinese and a Mexican. Each wore only a chemise and an inviting smile.

"Livery stable in town?" the Virginian asked, swinging down from the saddle immediately opposite the cathouse entrance.

"Six of them, stranger. Carly lives on men just passin' through. You come back to my place after you bedded down your horse?" She waved both arms to indicate the women in the windows. "All of them clean girls. In body, of course. Their minds, now, that's another matter!"

The madam shrieked with strident laughter. She had a series of double chins, but the thick shell of her makeup held them rigid while her obese body trembled under the fur coat.

"Any lawman in Carly?"

She laughed again, curtailed it, and spat at the hard packed ground in front of her feet. "That's one dirty word my girls don't speak, stranger! And if you want to stay out of trouble in Carly, you better not speak it too loud or too often."

"Grateful to you," Steele acknowledged, and touched the brim of his hat.

"You don't owe me nothin', stranger. Just anxious to keep trouble away from this town. Killin's ain't good for business." Another ugly laugh. "Dead men can't get laid—'cept six feet under the ground!"

"Yes, ma'am," Steele responded as he led his horse between the cat house and the cantina. "I guess the best whore in the world can't raise a dead man."

Shrill laughter followed him down the dark alley,

then was lost amid the countless other sounds of men and women enjoying the rip-roaring pleasures of the town without law.

The first livery stable he came to was four streets back from the plaza, at the end of a row of buildings offering games of chance, dancing girls and Chinese food. The sign above the door proclaimed: MCTAVISH'S FEED AND STABLING.

McTavish was an old-timer close to seventy, with a broad Scottish accent to match his name. He had an ancient desk beside a stove at the rear of the malodorous stable and was reading a newspaper in the dim light of a turned-low lamp. He had avaricious eyes and sucked on a piece of straw all the time. After demanding a dollar and a half in advance, he showed a broad grin composed of twinkling eyes and false dentures. He was firmly gentle in his handling of the weary piebald.

"Men come and go all the time here, son," he replied to Steele's question about the recent newcomers to Carly. "I only see the ones that bring their mounts to my stable. Or any that happen to be eating Chinese grub next door the same time I am."

Steele had slid the Colt Hartford from the boot. He watched the skinny old man stow his saddle and bedroll on a shelf alongside the gear of other men, and saw the grin fade as McTavish resumed his seat and raised his feet up on to the desk.

"Lot of men come here to raise hell, son. Because this is the wide-openest town in the southwest. I dunno, maybe in the whole country. More willing women, more kinds of gambling, more places to get drunk in and more kinds of everything."

"Except law, I've been told."

"You were told right, son. And that's another reason why a lot of men come here. Don't ask me which men or why exactly it's the lack of law as well as what we do have that brings them here. I don't ask questions. Nobody asks questions. Except the army patrols that swing through here every now and then. The army have learned to ask the right questions, son. And not to mind that they get the same answers all the time. Civilians who ask questions never get answers. Might get beaten up bad. Or run out of town. Sometimes killed." He picked up his newspaper. It was the *Santa Fe Journal*, yellow with age. On the floor close to his chair there was a stack of other newspapers and magazines which looked just as old. "We don't have law in Carly, son. But we do have rules."

"You're the exception to one of them?"

Steele had gone to the door. The old man squinted across at him, his expression serious as he shook his head. "I haven't told you anything about the ten men you're looking for, son. Just told you how to behave in Carly. Dead men or those that are run out of town don't bring me any profit."

"Grateful to you. Folks that answer questions get the same treatment as those that ask them—of the wrong folks?"

A nod. "Surely."

The Virginian had been pensive. Now he grinned. "So if I go into any place in town and ask my questions I'm in trouble."

"You're betting your life on it, son."

He lifted his newspaper and leaned close to it to read the faded print in the dim light.

"And if I mention your name, you're in trouble?"

McTavish hid behind his paper for stretched seconds. Then he lowered it slowly. By that time, Steele had crossed the stable and was standing immediately in front of the ancient desk; close enough to see the mixture of anger and fear in the strained eyes and the paleness of the age-wrinkled skin.

"I set you straight and you threaten to screw me up, son," McTavish accused. "You look like a decent

46

young man. Didn't think someone like you would be first."

"Nobody's tried it before?"

"Too stupid to think of it. Or too scared. Then again, perhaps nobody's ever looked for anybody in Carly before."

"Ten men? Can you help?"

"I'm disappointed in you, son. But I'm not scared of you. Scared of what others might do to me, though. If you spread lies about me. But I can't stop you. I go from here to the Chinese eating house and back again. All I do day and night. You're the first customer I've had in four days. And the last time I saw a strange face in the eating house was the night before last. Your move, son."

Steele pursed his lips and sighed. "Do I have to stay out of dark alleys, old-timer?"

The twinkling eyes and false teeth contributed to another bright grin. "Never killed a man in my life, son. Nor had one killed any which way. Your horse will be ready for you any time you want to pick him up. Two days pass without you showing up, I sell him to the Chinese eating house."

He raised the paper in front of his face again. Steele turned and headed for the door.

"Son!" McTavish called.

The Virginian halted abruptly, and turned slowly. The old man was still holding the *Sante Fe Journal* in one hand, flat on the desk top. His other hand was fisted around the butt of a Navy Colt. He must have taken it from a desk drawer, for he did not wear a gunbelt over his dungarees. He cocked the hammer and Steele froze in half turn, feeling the sweat of fear in his palms and at the small of his back.

"A stable ain't a dark alley, but I don't intend to shoot you. Could do, though. If I wanted."

Steele's fear had been controlled. Used to feed extra

47

tension into his muscles as he became poised to respond to whatever action McTavish took. Now he relaxed. "You've made your point, old-timer."

McTavish nodded and eased the hammer of the Colt back to the rest. Then he dropped the gun into a drawer of the desk. "A man is never too old to do that, son. If he keeps his wits about him. Nor to kill for the first time." He hid his face behind the newspaper again. "I'll be seeing you, son. If you don't make any more mistakes—around men with a less kindly disposition than me. If you do, I won't be at the funeral. Been at too many. That's something else Carly has more of than most other places, I guess. Unmarked graves. Spread all over everywhere."

"It figures, for a town laid out the way this one is," Steele muttered.

"What does, son?" The old man sounded disinterested.

"Not having a dead center."

CHAPTER FOUR

The Virginian ambled through the alleys and across the one-sided streets to the south end of town. It was close to midnight now and the weather was cold enough to lay a carpet of frost crystals over buildings and the intervening ground. But Carly showed no sign of closing down for the day. Lamplight continued to gleam from most windows and the noise remained constant, merely rising and falling in volume as doors were opened and closed to let out or admit customers who were spreading their patronage around the various places of entertainment.

Steele was totally ignored by the men—individuals, in pairs, threes and larger groups—who wandered from one place to another as he made his nonchalant way to the far end of town. It was as if the madam and her whores he had seen at the House of Pleasure on the plaza had been a living advertisement for the human melting pot that was Carly. There were whites on the streets and moving along the alleys. Negroes, Mexicans, Chinese, Indians. Some men had the appearance of just coming in off a thousand-mile cattle drive. Others would not have looked out of place in the plushest restaurants of San Francisco, New Orleans or New York. The Chinese wore coolie hats and the Indians were attired in buckskin leggings. Several Mexicans wore crossed bandoliers heavy with bullets. Except for the dudes, everyone wore a gun or a knife plainly in sight.

Only Steele carried a rifle—canted casually to his left shoulder—but neither this nor anything else about his appearance attracted more than an accidental glance in his direction.

A combination of glowing stoves and frosty weather caused every window to be misted by condensation. So, as he began to work his way back through the pleasure-bent town, he had to enter each noisy establishment to check on the people crowded inside. The polyglot mixture of those both supplying the services and pleasures and buying them was much as he had been led to expect by what he had already seen of the residents and visitors in Carly.

Again, he caused no stir. Carly was a town of many businesses and everybody minded their own. Bartenders glanced expectantly at him in saloons and cantinas. Waitresses, not pretty or willing enough to be whores, eyed him indifferently when he entered restaurants. At dancehalls, theatres and sideshows he paid the price of admission to attendants who were interested only in his money. The fact that he entered the places, stayed no longer than a minute or two and then left did not attract attention to him. And he guessed this was common practice for newcomers to town—to assess the potential of Carly before deciding where to spend money.

The only establishments he did not investigate were the bordellos, boarding houses and hotels, where questions would be necessary. If he did not strike pay dirt elsewhere, he would try them later.

He was a little more than halfway back to the plaza when he saw a familiar face—that of a young woman with dyed blonde hair and a full-blown figure he had last seen in Borderville. Then, she had struck a kitchen match to set fire to the kerosene-soaked hay bales behind the funeral parlor. Now, attired in a bright yellow, low-cut dress, her plump face over-painted and her hair

50

falling about her shoulders, she was serving drinks in O'Ryan's Saloon.

A platform at one end of the saloon was brightly lit, to show six near-naked Negresses dancing wildly to the jangling beat of a piano. The rest of the place was in gloom and as the Borderville widow moved back and forth between the bar and the crowded tables, she was a competing form of entertainment with the dancing troupe. Arms snaked through the darkened, over-heated, malodorous air to probe hands under the hem of her skirts or pinch fingers on her rump. Occasionally, as she leaned across tables to put down glasses and bottles, men cupped her breasts or pressed their sweating faces into the naked crook of her neck.

Because of the low level of light beyond the glow from the platform, it was impossible to see how much effort it cost the woman to match the lascivious hilarity of the men who pawed her.

Steele circled the saloon, then weaved among the tables, looking for the familiar face of a man and watchful for a sign that he had been seen and recognized from the meeting on the trail.

But none of the Sherrill bunch was in O'Ryan's. As he approached one end of the long bar, which had no standing customers while the show was in progress, the Borderville widow saw him, whirled and pointedly avoided looking at him again.

"Get you somethin', mister?" a bored-looking, bald-headed bartender asked, picking at his teeth with a split match.

"Somebody, feller. The owner."

The bartender started in on his nails with the match. "Buried O'Ryan this mornin', mister. From natural cause of old age. Before you make the joke I already heard ten times, O'Ryan dyin' ain't why we got black girls dancing. Nigger gash always been a speciality of the house."

The Borderville widow escaped the groping hands to place another order with a bartender at the far end of the counter. She kept her head firmly turned away from the Virginian. Steele pointed with his free hand toward her.

"She's white, feller."

The bartender didn't like his tone and he dropped his bored expression to show toughness. "A new speciality of the house. Workin' out real fine. Customers like it real fine. Maybe we'll get a whole string of female waitresses. If we can get them to work as cheap."

The woman was back among the men, submitting to the indignities of their public caresses as she balanced a tray of foaming glasses.

"Seems like she counts that kinda thing like a bonus on top of what she gets paid," the bartender growled, with a puzzled shake of his head. "Guess there ain't many females like her around." Then he got the hardness back into his eyes as he returned his attention to Steele. "Not that it's any damn business of yours, mister. You wanna drink, or you wanna leave?"

"Leave," the Virginian rasped. And added the lie: "With my wife."

The bartender was puzzled again, then vented a low gasp of understanding as Steele turned and moved along the counter to where the Borderville widow was running the gauntlet of reaching hands.

Up on the stage, the dancing girls continued to stomp in ill-matched time to the jangling beat of an out-of-tune piano. Yelling, laughing men beyond the distraction of the white woman devoted their drunken, lustful attention on the sweat-sheened black flesh of the dancers. The Borderville widow continued her play-acting, responding with flashing teeth and glinting eyes to the men who cupped, caressed and pinched her body. And she was not aware of the nearness of Steele until she

52

wrenched free of the hands and stepped onto the clear area between the tables and the counter.

The Virginian was standing immediately in front of her, his frame apparently relaxed but his face set in grim lines. The woman's forced mirth dried up and an angry glare widened her dark eyes.

"Get out of my way!" she snarled, pulling up short, then jerking to the side to try to go around him.

Steele reached out with his free hand and clenched it about her upper arm. The grip was tight enough to alter her yell of alarm into a shriek of pain. The men close by heard it and whirled toward Steele and the woman. Their shouts attracted the attention of other customers. Some of the girls on the stage saw the disturbance and broke step. The pianist faultered and the dance came to an untidy end.

"I want to do things my—" the Borderville widow shouted.

The raucous noise of the saloon had started to subside as liquor-sodden brains struggled to understand what was happening. Then there was an abrupt silence, as Steele jerked the woman toward him, released his hold on her arm, clenched his fist and crashed it against the side of her jaw.

Her enraged plea was curtailed and her sideways momentum strengthened the impact of the short punch. She was rigid in the first instant of unconsciousness. Then started to topple to the side, her body melting into limpness. The tin tray clattered to the floor and signaled an enraged outburst from the customers.

Steele powered down into a crouch and curled his free arm around the falling form. When he straightened, the Borderville widow was folded like a loosely packed sack of flour over his left shoulder. Held there as easily as he kept the Colt Hartford canted to the right one.

A sea of faces glared at him through the half dark-

53

ness and he smelled the foul breath that vented from every shouting, cursing mouth. The gloved forefinger of his right hand squeezed the rifle trigger the instant his thumb had cocked the hammer. He alone did not flinch as the gunshot cracked out, bringing another silence to the crowded room. Shock was mixed with the rage now.

"He claims she's his wife!" the bald-headed bartender yelled from the far end of the counter.

Steele, his expression impassive, nodded in confirmation. "Trouble with her," he said. "Don't want to with anybody else, unless they've a mind to start it."

"Start the music!" the bartender ordered. "Get them blacks dancin' again."

The pianist began to beat out the jangling tune. The dance restarted, but with less enthusiasm than before. Steele turned and moved down the clear area between the counter and the crowded tables. Most of the customers accepted the situation and quickly forgot their disappointment as they cheered the dancers back to a frenzy of lewd action and yelled for glasses to be filled.

The Virginian ignored his surroundings until two men rose from a table close to the entrance and drifted lazily across to block the doorway. Both were in their early twenties, tall and broad and arrogantly confident as they faced the compactly built, heavily burdened Steele. They were dressed Western-style and toted Colt revolvers in tied down holsters.

"A weddin' don't make a woman a slave," the heavier man on the left said, shouting to be heard above the raucous sound of the saloon. "Me and Danny figure that's so."

"Sure do, don't we, George," Danny growled.

Both men held their right hands hovering close to the jutting butts of their holstered Colts.

Steele came to a halt ten feet in front of them. He pursed his lips and sighed. With eyes that expressed a lazy look, he surveyed the men. Their faces were red

54

with the effects of liquor and their eyes were glazed. They were unsteady on their feet.

"Means there's a difference of opinion between us," the Virginian allowed. "No sweat on my part. You want to make an issue of it?"

"Talks fancy, don't he?" George said with a slack-mouthed grin.

"Yeah," Danny agreed, and spat at the floor. "Throw's a fancy punch as well, don't he? When there's a woman on the end of it."

Steele nodded. "You want to make an issue of it."

He bent slowly at the knees and waist, canting forward to allow the unconscious woman to slide off his shoulder. He steadied her so that she reached the floor gently. He side-stepped away from her as he straightened, the rifle still sloped to his right shoulder.

Danny and George moved forward from the door, emphasizing their confidence in the brightness of their grins.

Steele tipped the rifle away from his right shoulder and allowed it to fall to the side, half stopping as if to lay it on the floor.

The grins of Danny and George became broader and they raised their hands up from the holstered Colts, clenching their fists.

Steele sensed a wave of attention sweep away from the dancing girls to be directed toward the tableau at the doorway. The men facing him were also aware of the watching eyes.

The Virginian waited until the youngsters made the mistake of interrupting their concentration on him to check on the size of their audience, then altered the swing of the Colt Hartford. Still gripping it around the frame, he halted the sideways movement, twisted his wrist to point the rifle straight ahead, and lunged forward.

The muzzle drove hard into the soft flesh of Danny's

lower belly. The man shrieked his pain and folded forward, unclenching both fists and clawing at the source of his pain. He staggered backward and hit the door.

Abruptly, the dancing girls lost every member of their audience as all eyes swung toward the doorway. The sounds of excitement rose in volume as the new brand of entertainment was presented.

George expressed surprise, then rage. He screamed a curse and went for his gun.

Steele jerked back on the rifle and released it, so that it skittered along the floor behind him. He was still in a half-crouch. The hand which had released the rifle came forward, delved into the gaping split in his pants leg, and emerged clasping the knife.

Danny was on his knees, recovering from the initial agony of the blow. He saw the knife flash in the lamplight and went for his gun.

Both youngsters had sobered fast, shocked out of their drunken arrogance by the smooth speed of the Virginian.

"No killin'!" the bald-headed bartender shrieked, his voice cutting stridently across the bedlam of noise in the saloon.

George had his gun clear of the holster. Danny's Colt was still in the leather, but his hand was fisted around it. Steele turned sideways onto both men, his right foot coming up off the floor. The knee was bent, then straightened. The heel of his boot slammed into Danny's nose. There was the crack of breaking gristle and then a moist-sounding scream as blood weltered into the back of the injured man's throat. Danny went backward again, cracking his head against the door.

The noise of bone against wood was masked by a scream from George.

As Steele slammed his damaging foot back to the floor, he became solidly balanced. His free hand

56

"All set!" he called, his voice tense with controlled excitement.

Down at the foot of the slope, lines of lamplight showed at the slit windows of the church. No other building in Borderville was illuminated from within. Sherrill nudged his horse forward in a slow walk. The big stallion did not break stride as the rope became taut with the burden of the dead weight tied to it.

The half moon had been a patch of paleness in the northern sky before the sun set. Now it gleamed bright with a blue light that seemed to intensify the whiteness of the adobe buildings. The shadows it caused were darker than those created by the sun earlier.

The singing sounded sweeter in the night, masking the slow beat of hooves against hard-packed dirt and sun-bleached rock, the creak of saddle leather, the jingle of spurs—and the slithering of flesh down the hillside.

The dead man at the end of the rope was naked. He had been old enough to die—close to eighty—but no man of any age would have wished to die the way he did. Both his hands had been axed off at the wrists and his feet had been severed at the ankles. A skilfully wielded knife had disemboweled him and cut his heart out of his chest. Rigor mortis was long gone and the limpness of the corpse's arms and legs was due equally to death and to broken bones. The grimace of agony on his wrinkled face indicated that he had been a tough old man, that the nonfatal injuries had been inflicted first and he had had the stamina to endure them.

The rope was noosed around his unfeeling neck. There was no more liquid blood in the body and the corpse left no staining in its wake. Just an impression of its passing in the dust, which was soon obliterated by the hooves of the nine horses and the unladen burro which trailed behind.

At the foot of the slope, no words were exchanged,

6

Across flat scrub desert for five miles, then through rocky hills. Mesas featured the desert, along with many varieties of cactus, clumps of mesquite and patches of greasewood.

Nothing moved out there in the desert—except the shadows of rock and vegetation, stretching further east as the sun began to hide its trailing half.

"Gettin' away oughta be real easy, Mr. Sherrill," Bergen said in a wise tone.

"Never steered your father wrong, Thad. Nor any of the others."

"Damn it, he'd have liked it real good to be with you again. The stories he used to tell me about ridin' with you in Kansas and Missouri. I used to—"

The pump-organ started up again and then the voices of the congregation all but masked the accompaniment.

"Ancient history, boy!" Sherrill cut in on Bergen. "Happy for you to think about it. I'm not going back that far right now."

"Here we are, Mr. Sherrill."

Wheeler Mitchell was a short and skinny man of thirty-five with a black patch over one eye and crooked teeth. His unconcealed eye was coal black and surveyed the world with a glaring intensity. He had replaced his Bowie knife in a sheath at the small of his back and as he spoke he jerked powerfully on a length of rope and handed the free end to Sherrill.

The gaunt-faced leader of the group accepted the rope, fed it under his right leg and had enough slack to lash it securely to his saddle-horn. The sun was set now, with only a crimson glow above the western ridges to hold back the night. The air felt a lot colder. The smell of death was stronger.

Sherrill nodded and Mitchell turned quickly and returned to the hollow to mount his horse. Bergen wheeled his stallion and went to join the others.

streaked across in front of his body, folded around the barrel of George's gun, and forced it high. At the same time, his knife hand whipped upward and the point of the knife drove deep into the armpit of his assailant. Then, when George continued to grip the Colt and struggled to get it down to the aim, Steele appeared to submit to a superior strength.

He allowed his left hand to be forced down and seemed only capable of ducking away from the threat of the revolver muzzle. But his right hand did not surrender. It withdrew the knife until just an inch of blade was sunk in George's flesh. Then he jerked it toward him. Jacket and shirt sleeve and human tissue were sliced with consummate ease. George opened his hand from around the gun butt as his arm was gashed open; bone deep from top to bottom, the blade not pulled clear until it had cut through the fleshy base of his thumb.

George staggered backward and leaned against the door, groaning and squeezing tears from his eyes as he ran his left hand up and down the length of his right arm, trying to stem the massive flow of blood.

Steele whirled into a crouch, facing Danny and brandishing the knife against another possible attack. But Danny was still huddled on the floor, both hands cupped over his broken nose.

The excitement of the audience died. The sounds made by the injured men were all that disturbed the tense silence for a moment. Then the Borderville widow groaned her intention to regain consciousness.

Steele felt the sweat of fear dry on the palms of his hands inside his gloves. But stove heat and the after-effects of exertion kept the pores of his face wide-open. He kicked George's Colt under a nearby table. Danny vented a gasp of terror as the Virginian leant over him. But Steele merely lifted the gun from the man's holster, scaled it across the floor in front of the counter, and wiped the knife blade clean of blood on his greasy hair. He slid the weapon back into the boot sheath on the way to coming erect.

He retrieved the Colt Hartford and slipped it to his shoulder before he raked his cold-eyed glare around the customers and bartenders. Aware that his actions and the look on his face were a sufficient warning, he kept his tone even. "Anybody else want this woman that badly?" he asked, with a nod toward the two injured youngsters.

"Take her and clear out, mister!" the bald-headed bartender growled. "Carly's full of women. Ain't no reason to fight over one of them." There were nods and grunts of agreement from the customers.

"Didn't you know that?" Steele asked George and Danny.

The Borderville widow groaned again when Steele stooped, grasped her right wrist, and started to drag her toward the doorway.

"The rest all cost money!" Danny snarled, his breathing ragging through his smashed, bloody nose. He hauled himself to his feet and scuttled across the threshold to help the more badly injured George out of Steele's path.

"Damn right!" a man said from among the seated customers. "Your wife made it plain she was anybody's for nothin', mister! That ain't never been known in this town before!"

"Must mean she was kept real short at home, I guess!" another man yelled, and was rewarded with a gust of scornful laughter.

Steele held the rifle under his arm to open the door. Night air streamed into the saloon to cool his sweat-sheened face.

"Yeah, a big man with what he's got in his right boot," George rasped between teeth clenched against pain. "But real small between the legs, seems like."

"Quit it!" Danny warned him. "You thinkin' about what's between a man's legs got us in enough trouble for one night."

He glanced fearfully toward Steele, who responded with an easy grin as he refastened a grip on the woman's wrist. "Good advice, feller. For a man with hard feelings. Reckon you might have to do more than talk to him, though. His right arm being in such bad shape."

Danny eyed the Virginian quizzically as Steele dragged the Borderville widow over the threshold.

"Might have to take him in hand."

CHAPTER FIVE

Danny slammed the door on Steele, as the bald-headed bartender yelled for the music and dancing to resume. Outside in the cold night, the Virginian rested his rifle, raised the groaning woman upright against the wall of the saloon and slung her over his shoulder again. Then he retrieved the Colt Hartford and back-tracked down two alleys until he found the Barnard's Inn which he had bypassed previously.

The frost was thick and hard now and white crystals began to form on his coat and the woman's dress as he made the short journey. The bitter cold of the new day's early hours was keeping most people off the streets of Carly. The few men he did see showed no more interest in him than others had earlier.

The inn was a long, low building of adobe with a gaming house on one side of it and a theatre on the other. The theatre was closed and the gambling joint was in the process of putting up the shutters for the night. From elsewhere in town came noises to indicate that a few places were still doing as good business as O'Ryan's.

Steele had to rouse a sleeping Mexican who was sprawled across a desk in the tiny lobby of the hotel. He was young and fat and his breath smelled of chili and whisky. His eyes looked at Steele and the obviously distressed woman with a total lack of interest.

"A double, *señor*?" he asked after a gaping yawn.

60

"Single. I won't be staying long."

"I must charge for a double, *señor*. Two people go to a room, I must charge for a double. I just work here, *señor*. You will pay five dollar."

The Borderville widow began to move as well as groan. Steele rested his rifle, took out his bankroll and peeled off a five. The clerk was suddenly wide awake and very interested when he saw the wad of bills go back into Steele's pocket.

"If your lady friend she is no good, *señor*," he said as he fished a key from under the desk, "I can arrange for another. Fine woman. Cheap charge. My cousin twice removed."

Steele picked up the Colt Hartford and rested it on the desk top, muzzle two inches from the Mexican's bulging belly. "Five dollars is all I pay, feller. You try any way to get more money out of me, it will be wrong. Dead wrong."

The Mexican gulped. "*Si, señor*." Another gulp as the rifle was canted to the shoulder. "It is last room on left along hallway. You will not be disturbed, *señor*."

"I'm already disturbed," the Virginian muttered as he turned and tightened his grip around the struggling woman.

The hallway was in pitch darkness. Steele felt his way ahead with the Colt Hartford jutting out in front of him. The sounds of deep breathing and snoring filtered out into the cold hallway from the rooms on either side.

"Put me down, you beast!" the Borderville widow shrieked, beating on the base of Steele's spine with the sides of her fists.

"Be quiet, lady," he told her. "Time for talking will be very soon."

He found the end wall of the hall, back-tracked, and tilted to the side as he released his hold on the woman. She vented a shriek of alarm as she fell, then a cry of pain as she hit the hard floor on her hands and knees. Steele swung open the door of the room he had been given. Several disgruntled voices yelled out demands for quiet.

He struck a match on the doorframe and held it out, so that he was able to see the woman and she could see him. "Women who act like whores deserve to get treated like them, ma'am," he said softly, impassive in response to the fear and hatred directed at him from her dark eyes. "I've got an inbred respect for ladies. The southerner in me, I reckon. Your choice."

There was a dark bruise on the side of her jaw where he had hit her. Her over-painted face was streaked with dirt from when she had been dumped on the saloon floor.

"I can scream real loud!" she hissed.

Steele allowed the match to fall to the floor. Then he stooped, hooked a hand inside the low-cut neckline of her dress and jerked her to her feet. She caught her breath, perhaps to power a scream. But Steele's words silenced her.

"You'll be out cold, lady. Just like last time. Reckon I can placate the complainers by offering you around at a couple of bucks a time."

She let out her breath with just a frightened whistling sound. Then her breasts began to rise and fall quickly against Steele's knuckles.

"You would, too," she rasped.

"Right, ma'am. You screw me one way, I make sure you get screwed lots of ways."

"Let me go."

Steele did so, but with a slight shove that directed her across the threshold and into the room. It was at the rear of the hotel and the window was not draped, so that light from a saloon across the street filtered in to faintly illuminate the bare floor, narrow bed and a dresser constructed of old crates.

When the Virginian closed the door, the woman

hugged herself and stood stock still in the center of the tiny room. Her perfume masked whatever odors previous guests had left.

"Five horses were ridden out of town before I left this morning," Steele said softly, remaining by the door.

"But there are more than five of us who don't trust you, Steele," the woman hissed.

"One question answered, ma'am. So five rode north. Any more leave in any other direction? Or any more plan to come this way?"

"You mind your business and we'll mind ours."

"We're in the same business, ma'am. Finding Clyde Sherrill and his bunch."

"Not all of us want just that," she countered, her voice losing some of its timbre of stubbornness. "The women want them taken back to Borderville to hang."

"You ladies are going to hang them. My job is to find them and return them to you."

It was almost as cold inside the unheated hotel as out in the frosty night. The woman felt it more severely than Steele, dressed as she was in the revealing gown. She gasped and stepped out of the way as he crossed the room. But he ignored her until he had pulled a blanket off the bed. Still afraid, she allowed him to drape the blanket around her bare shoulders. Then she sat on the bed as he went to gaze out of the window.

She broke the prolonged silence, seemingly challenged to do so by his unmoving back. "We were distraught. After what happened. Margery Salisbury has always been the leader among the women in our town. When she called the meeting and put it to us that we should ask your help, we all agreed. But later, after we had time to think, some of us realized we had no reason to trust you. You came to town a stranger. You talked tough and showed us not one whit of sympathy for the tragedy we suffered. You were totally uninterested in us until you were offered money. Then you rode out again

63

and we had no way of knowing if you would even attempt to do the job we set you."

She massaged her bruised jaw as she spoke. Her tone was weary now and she spoke as if she was resigned and even uncaring.

"So some of us decided to take matters into our own hands. And we came to this place of sin, which is known throughout the southwest for the pleasures it offers men with money. And as a refuge for those who have come by the money dishonestly. All of us know Sherrill. And we also know the faces of a Mexican and a man with an eye patch who kept us captive in the church while the slaughter took place."

Steele turned his back on the window now and rested his rump on the sill. "The women who didn't trust me, ma'am? They all out of the Borderville cat house?"

She vented a shocked gasp. "There is no such place in Borderville, sir!" Then the rigidity drained out of her and she hunched her shoulders under the blanket and hung her head, her posture one of misery. Her tone became flat and weary again. "The five of us who came to Carly are all respectable women. I and Mrs. Finn and Mrs. James were married to hard-working miners. Mrs. James is the widow of a fine man who taught school in Borderville. Joan Ricter assisted her husband in running the grocery store."

She raised her head to look at Steele and spread an expression of grim determination across her overpainted face. "Think what you will of us, Mr. Steele. But we knew our best chance to find the men we are seeking was to frequent the places where such men were likely to be. And, because we are women, we were forced to demean ourselves in such a place as Carly. I can assure you that none of us is enjoying the experience. But we will go to any lengths to bring the murderers to justice."

Her posture became deflated again and she looked

64

ready to keel over and sprawl in exhaustion across the narrow bed.

"Big decision to take, ma'am," Steele allowed. "Ready to take another one?"

She moved her head slowly to look expectantly at him.

"Either you go back to the saloon and, along with the others who don't trust me, do things your way. Or, you round up the other widows, head back for your home town and leave me to get on with the job I've been paid to do. Be grateful you come to the decision fast, ma'am. Night's growing old and if there's a lead in this town, I'd like to find it before dawn."

He crossed the room and halted with his gloved hand on the doorknob. He looked back over his shoulder at her.

"If we stay here?" she asked, a little fearfully.

Steele sighed and turned to lean his back against the door. "I'm a mean bastard, ma'am. There isn't the time to tell you how I became that way. And maybe even if I told you, you wouldn't find in it any reason why I should be the way I am. So I'll just tell you about Borderville and me."

He pursed his lips and in the pale moonlight filtering through the dirty window of the room his face looked very youthful, showing a pensive expression. He was silent for a few moments, as if he was thinking how to phrase what was in his mind, or perhaps trying to understand it himself before offering it to the woman.

"Last time I had a really bad thing happen to me, I went to Mexico, ma'am. I escaped the law there. And tried to escape the past. I got drunk there and stayed drunk for a long time. Didn't do anything for me except put me off alcohol for life."

He was staring into the infinity that stretched away from the darkest corner of the mean room. But he could

65

sense the woman's eyes on him and felt she had set aside her own trouble in an effort to understand his.

"I've had a lot of bad experiences since then," the Virginian continued. "Not many good ones. But they never affected me the same way as the one that took me down to Mexico. I was heading across the border though, when I rode into your town. Not intending to get drunk. Not running from the law. Just riding. And looking for something, I reckon.

"Thought I'd found it in Borderville. Found plenty of death, which is nothing new to me. But I did two things I'd never done before when there was a stink of trouble in the air, ma'am. Two things you won't understand but which mean a lot to me."

He held out his rifle, fisted in his gloved hands. The moonlight showed the dark charred patches on the rosewood stock of the Colt Hartford—scars from the fire which had raised the Virginian plantation house—and glinted on the gold plate which bore the inscription: TO BENJAMIN P. STEELE, WITH GRATITUDE—ABRAHAM LINCOLN.

"Never put on the gloves and, for a time, didn't carry the rifle." He slanted the weapon—his sole inheritance from his father—back to his shoulder. "Those two things meant I had a feeling for Borderville, ma'am. A good one. And I reckoned that maybe I had been riding for Mexico to look for a good feeling."

He rasped the back of his free hand along the bristles of his jaw.

"You made no offer to help us," the woman said.

"Bad habits die hard," he responded with a cold grin. "I'm not the helping kind, unless there's a price tag. But, you know something? Two hundred and thirty-one dollars wasn't enough. And if I got back and kept every cent that was taken from the Borderville Bank, even that wouldn't have been enough.

"Two things headed me back north, ma'am. Two offers I didn't take up. First all that jewelry that must mean a great deal to the women. Second, the invitation that I could bed down with any woman that took my fancy. Been just one woman who was prepared to share my bed, it wouldn't have meant much. But every woman in town . . . that's what finally sold me. A man can't just ride on through a town like that, especially when he has a good feeling about it anyway. This man couldn't.

"And now I'm sold even harder, ma'am. After what you and the others who came here have done."

He glanced toward her as she opened her mouth to speak. But his raised hand silenced her. "You didn't need to prove yourselves to me. But it seems I have to do something to earn your trust. Which I can't do until I deliver the Sherrill bunch to Borderville."

"Words help, Mr. Steele," the woman said softly. "When spoken from the heart." She stood up from the bed, still holding the blanket tightly around her. "May I finish speaking for you? You felt the need to protect us after our tragedy. To protect us from the results of the steps we were prepared to take to bring Sherrill and the others to justice. But you will not contribute to our cause further if we lift a finger to help ourselves?"

"It's lifting your skirts that bothers me, ma'am," Steele corrected, and drew a gasp of shock from the woman, as if she had totally detached herself from what she had been doing when he found her in the saloon. "If you had been whores yesterday, I'd have been in Mexico by now."

He turned and swung open the door.

"Wait!" she called, and hurried across the room. "I'll have to talk with the others." She rested a hand lightly on his forearm. "And I am sure they'll be as anxious as I am to finish with Carly and put the shame of it behind them."

67

He stood back to allow her out of the room ahead of him, then trailed her.

"You won't wait?" she asked, startled.

"In the mission at the north end of town, ma'am. Or maybe you'll have to wait for me—until I've finished checking for the Sherrill bunch."

Out in the dimly lit lobby, she nodded in acknowledgment. The Mexican at the desk was still trying to get to sleep again after Steele had roused him. He raised his head from the desk top and his eyes were glazed for a few moments. Then snapped wide.

"You are not staying the night, *señor*? You have complaint against the accommodation provided?" He sounded like a man whose pride had been severely injured. "It will be my pleasure to give you the double room you paid for, *señor*." His big eyes switched to the Borderville widow and expressed tacit admiration as they roamed over her full-blown figure. "Your friend, she is much *señorita* for such a small bed."

The woman vented a grunt of disgust and glared at the Mexican. "All I did was sit on it!" she snapped.

The clerk's eyes became quizzical as they moved toward Steele.

The Virginian shrugged, then showed his youthful grin. "She didn't trust me, feller. Looking for ten other men."

CHAPTER SIX

Carly was a good deal quieter now and, as Steele continued to work his way northward from O'Ryan's Saloon, there were few places still open. Those that were generated little of the earlier excitement. Business in saloons, gaming houses and bordellos was slack, ticking over with contributions from men either too weary or too drunk to raise even the slightest kind of hell.

Steele saw no familiar faces until he had crossed the plaza and entered the derelict mission church adjacent to the abandoned fort. The Borderville widow had left him outside the hotel and, without him noticing, she had found her companions and assembled them on the frost-layered floor of the roofless church.

As he moved through the arched entrance, he sensed excitement in the chill air, and he also felt an aura of camaraderie directed toward him from the women grouped close to an overturned font. It was obvious the woman he had taken out of O'Ryan's had given the others a full report of her conversation with Steele—and that they had been swayed by her conviction that he could be trusted.

She rattled off their names in rapid speed, pointing a trembling hand at each in turn. The Virginian recognized three from seeing them in Borderville.

"Great news, Mr. Steele!" the still unnamed woman he had taken from the saloon announced when the in-

69

troductions were completed. "Mrs. Ricter has seen the man with the eye patch."

Joan Ricter was the most attractive of the group. A pretty brunette in her early twenties with wide eyes and slender figure. She was bursting with the need to make the report herself and ran the words into each other when she received a nod from Steele.

"He came into the Crystal Ballroom where I was workin' and when he left I was able to slip away and follow him but I couldn't keep up with him and when I got back one of the girls who works at the place all the time told me his name is Wheeler Mitchell and that he's the undertaker in Carly."

She sucked in a deep breath, but the aging and still-handsome Mrs. Amelia Finn spoke first.

"He lives behind his place of business, Mr. Steele. That's toward the south side of—"

"Know where it is ma'am," Steele cut in. "And I'm grateful to all you ladies for your help. Best you get your horses and ride back to Borderville now."

Joan Ricter and Linda Chambers looked as if they were about to object. But they were given no opportunity by the woman from O'Ryan's.

"Certainly, Mr. Steele. All the ladies have complete faith in you. And all apologize for doubting you at first—and thank you for making it unnecessary for us to remain in this godless, sinful place. Get to your work. And rely on us to return to Borderville."

The nods of agreement seemed to be overemphatic which gave them a forced quality. But Steele said nothing. He merely sighed, touched his hat brim and went out of the mission and across the plaza.

There were no women in the windows of the House of Pleasure now. The windows were dark and the door was firmly closed. The places on either side of the bordello were also shut for the night. He felt the gazes of the Borderville widows on his back, but the women made no move to leave the church.

Two men advertised themselves as morticians in Carly. Mitchell's premises were four streets back from the plaza. All four buildings on the street were of a similar construction: timber with flat roofs and porches. A door at the center of each with a display window on either side. There was a hardware store, a bakery and the undertaking parlor with a gunsmith's on the other side of it. The three stores displayed samples of their wares in the windows. In Mitchell's windows were sample tombstones set against black velvet.

Steele stepped up on to the porch and rapped his knuckles on the one-piece wooden door. He waited until footsteps sounded on the other side and a moving lamp threw dancing shafts of light into the display windows. Then he turned his back on the door.

"Who is it? What d'you want this time of night?" There was new sleep and old liquor in Wheeler Mitchell's voice, clearly audible under the tone of irritation.

"Name's Steele," the Virginian answered, injecting a disguising gruffness into his own voice. "Want to make arrangements for a funeral."

"Can't it wait until mornin', mister?"

"Afraid not."

Bolts were slid and a key was turned in the lock. Steele was facing front again when the door swung open, with the Colt Hartford angled up from the hip to aim at the mortician's heart.

"Your funeral, you see," the Virginian said softly, and stepped across the threshold.

Mitchell's short and skinny frame was clothed in a loose-fitting nightshirt buttoned to the throat and reaching his ankles. At first, he was afraid only of the pointing rifle. Then his good eye looked into Steele's face. He thought he recognized the features, raised the lamp higher, then was certain. His fear expanded. He stepped

71

back into the funeral parlor as Steele advanced on him.

"On the trail," he croaked. "Out of Borderville. After we . . ."

The lamp began to sway as his body trembled. Steele was far enough inside to back-heel the door closed.

"You want to put that lamp down on the desk, feller? Borderville women reckon hanging is the most fitting way for a killer to die."

The lamplight glinted as brightly on his shiny patch as on his coal-black good eye. Then his teeth gleamed in a crafty smile. "So I got no fear of you blastin' me, mister?"

"Your life's the bet, feller. In the pot is the way it ends. I win the side stakes whether you cash in with a bullet or a rope. Or even a fire. You want to put the lamp down."

Wheeler Mitchell took two backward steps and did as he was told. His tongue darted out to lick his lips. Too much moisture trickled out of his mouth and he wiped his chin with the back of a hand.

"I reckon I can better any offer them women made you, Steele. Bank money divided even. I don't need it. I never did."

"I heard the burying business was a good one in Carly, feller. Get the money."

Mitchell started a grin, then realized the comment could not be regarded as acceptance of his offer. "It's in the bedroom."

"Won't take advantage of you," Steele told him, starting across the room.

As he followed the one-eyed man, he turned up the lamp wick. Enough light filtered through the doorway to show the spartanly furnished living room. In the bedroom, which was off to one side, there was just moonlight. But enough of it to show the bed, dresser, closet and chair. Mitchell's clothes were heaped on the chair with his gunbelt at the top. When the mortician glanced toward the chair, Steele made a clucking sound with his tongue against his teeth.

"You might get a better chance later, feller."

Mitchell scowled as he crouched at the side of the bed and reached beneath it. "That means I need one, uh? You'll take the money and still hand me over to them women?"

"How much a share worth, feller?"

"Five grand. One rich town, Borderville." He dragged a tin chest out from under the bed, sprung open the lid and stood back.

"Close it and sit on it, feller."

Mitchell swallowed hard and complied with the order. He licked his lips again as Steele approached him. This time he did not bother to wipe the spittle from his chin. "There's more than that in the box, Steele. Jewelry, gold fillin's outta teeth. Stuff from stiffs come my way. You can have it all."

"How about money?" the Virginian asked as he halted with the Colt Hartford muzzle a foot from Mitchell's good eye.

A shake of the head. "All the spare cash I get I sent to San Francisco. Honest truth. Figure to retire there when I've got enough. But I can fix it for you to get as much as you want."

Steele shook his head. "Just want to be sure I'm not taking more than I'm entitled to. Where's the others?"

"Others?"

"Nine others. One's named Clyde Sherrill."

A scowl replaced the anxious expression on the thin face of the one-eyed man. He pressed his lips tightly together, then voiced what the gesture signified. "No way you're gonna get me to tell you that, Steele. Do whatever the hell you can think up to me. But I owe those men too much."

"More than five thousand?"

Mitchell made to wave a hand, but then realized the

73

movement might be taken as an attempt to knock away the rifle barrel. "The bank money was a bonus. Ain't one of us bunch wouldn't have ridden with Clyde even if there wasn't a cent in it for us. More than that. Would have chipped in our own cash if he needed it to swing the job."

"Just went along for the killing, uh?"

Now a scornful grimace contorted the thin face. "Sure, Steele. Because Clyde wanted them people killed. If he'd wanted us to swim the friggin' Pacific Ocean to China, we'd have done that, too."

"War buddies, I reckon?"

"Damn right. All except the kid. And he's the boy of a man who didn't live long enough to help out Clyde. We was called Sherrill's Raiders around Kansas and Missouri way. But that ain't tellin' you not a thing, 'cause folks only knew Clyde's name. Nobody never did put handles to the men who followed Clyde."

"Grateful for the information," Steele said evenly. "You can get up now."

While he was talking about Sherrill's Raiders the man had relived vivid memories of the past and they had insulated him from his present fear. The Virginian's softly drawled words started him trembling again.

"It ain't that easy?" he croaked.

"Nothing worthwhile ever is, feller. I reckon the hardest thing in the world is to die with dignity. Get up." He backed away from Mitchell, picked up the man's gunbelt and tossed it into a corner. It landed heavily, weighty with the holstered revolver and sheathed knife. "Get dressed."

Mitchell had trouble getting out of his nightshirt and into his day clothes. Convinced Steele intended more than to simply take him back to Borderville, he continued to tremble. But his voice became more evenly pitched as he launched into a defense of the Sherrill bunch's actions.

74

"You only heard the women's version, Steele. But they didn't tell you everythin', I bet. Clyde ain't never denied he held up the Borderville bank and run down them kids. But it was an accident, he says. And men who know him well know he never lies. The kids, they run into his path and he tried to ride around 'em. He didn't make it."

He paused to glance at the Virginian and saw that he had an attentive listener. "Clyde was ready to face the rap of bank robbery. Meant prison, but he could take that. But the kids gettin' killed, that was an accident, not murder like them Borderville folks said. He tried to get that legal. Him and his wife both. But after Borderville brought in that guilty verdict, there was no way to do it. Not by no new trial in Tucson. So he busted free of them lawmen. And he was ready to forget what happened—much as a man can forget when he's gotta spend the rest of his life hidin' from the law."

Mitchell was fully dressed now, except for a topcoat and hat. They weren't in the bedroom.

"Get the money," Steele instructed. "Just the five thousand."

The one-eyed man bent over the box.

"I ain't finished yet," he complained, then lost the whine from his voice when Steele did not cut him off. "You heard most of that from the women, I bet. But no way they told you about Clyde's wife and kid."

"Told me he had a family," Steele responded as Mitchell straightened, his arms filled with bundles of bills. "Wrap them in a blanket, feller."

"When them Borderville folks heard they'd lost Clyde, they killed his wife and kid, Steele! Didn't tell you that, did they?"

"You didn't, did you, ladies?" Steele posed, with a fast glance toward the doorway.

He couldn't see the women; it wasn't his eyes which had supplied the evidence of their entry into the mortician's premises. First, as the Virginian had reached the chair and tossed away the gunbelt, he had felt a slight—almost imperceptible—drop in temperature as air from outside streamed into the building. Then the door between the display windows had been closed. Silently. But a rustle of petticoats had marked the course of the intruders across the office and into the living room. They were in there now, out of Steele's field of vision through the doorway.

"What?" Wheeler Mitchell rasped.

"I suppose you could say we killed them," the woman from O'Ryan's said dully as she stepped through the doorway. Joan Ricter was immediately behind her.

The mortician's fear expanded to terror when he saw the women—to such an extent he looked on the verge of panic. For a moment he was petrified and Steele recognized it as a prelude to recklessness.

"Aiming at your belly now, feller," the Virginian told him evenly. "A bullet there could kill you. If it doesn't you'll wish it had—every step of the way back to Borderville."

The softly spoken words penetrated the terror and when the rigidity drained from Mitchell, the man simply dropped into a sitting posture on the bed. He continued to cradle the money in his arms.

"We drove them out of town," the woman with dyed blonde hair went on. "It took a month. We just ignored her. Pretended she wasn't there. Made her step around us on the street. Or step out of the way when we came along. When she used up what money she had, she wasn't given any credit at the stores. After a month, she was broke. In more ways than one. Had no money to buy food for herself and the child, nor for the stage fare. So she started out walking north, carrying her baby. They were found two days later—dead from hunger. Exhaustion, maybe. Or exposure; hot sun by day and real cold by night."

Her tone was dull and uncaring. But, when Steele shot a glance at her, he saw that her eyes were bright with hatred as she glared at Mitchell.

"We didn't mean for her to die," the younger, prettier woman added defensively. "We just wanted for her to leave town. Because she was the one who got help for her husband so he could escape hanging for what he did. But she was a stubborn one, Dorrie Sherrill. She stayed too long."

"Waiting to hear from her husband, I reckon," Steele said.

"What she said," the blonde confirmed. "What happened to her going to change things, Mr. Steele?"

The Virginian shook his head. "No, ma'am. Only concerned with what Sherrill did to Borderville. What caused him to do it is no business of mine."

The woman from O'Ryan's nodded vigorously. "That's good. All right to take this killer back to Borderville now? It's why we stayed. To save you interrupting your work. We can take him and you can go on looking for the others."

"Sounds like a fine arrangement," Steele allowed. "You want to tie him up? Just his hands behind his back, I reckon."

The two women went to work like experts of long standing. Never coming between the aimed rifle and Mitchell, they tore a sheet into strips, ordered the man to drop the money, and lashed his wrists together at the small of his back. Then they looped and tied strips of sheet around his arms and body at chest and waist.

Fear seemed to have drained all but a meager reserve of his strength. The women had to help him to his feet. He licked his lips constantly, but there was no saliva on his tongue. It was obvious he feared the women more than Steele.

"Take the money with you," the Virginian instructed as he canted the Colt Hartford to his shoulder and eased the hammer to rest. "Find his coat and drape it over his shoulders."

They went out of the bedroom, across the living room and into the office. Mitchell swayed as he walked on stiff legs. Mrs. Ricter carried the blanket-wrapped money. The blonde gripped Mitchell's arm, steering him. She located his topcoat and hat on a hook just inside the front door. She put them on him.

"What if he starts yelling in town?" the blonde asked.

"He's a human being, ma'am. Like all of us, he believes that while there's life there's hope. If he yells hope will run out with the blood he spills."

"A shot will wake the whole town," Joan Ricter pointed out.

Steele bent his right knee, reached into the gaping slit and drew the knife. He showed it to the women and Mitchell before dropping his hand to his side. "More than one way to kill somebody," he drawled. "As you ladies know."

Mrs. Ricter went outside first, then Steele. The blonde brought up the rear, urging the frightened Wheeler Mitchell ahead of her. The younger and prettier woman continued to take the lead; back through the now deserted alleys and across the empty streets. Lights showed at windows here and there but the night was as quiet as it was cold. Their footfalls crunched frost. The mortician breathed noisily through his nose, as if fearful of opening his mouth and the action be mistaken.

There were three saddled horses in the church.

"The other three ladies?" Steele asked.

"Not here any more," the blonde supplied. "We would appreciate it if you'd lift the murderer on to a horse."

"In a while," the Virginian answered, pushing his rifle into the hands of the surprised woman and moving close to Mitchell. "Don't know yet whether he'll be sitting in the saddle or slumped across it."

78

"What—?" Mrs. Ricter asked.

"Shut up, ma'am." He spoke sharply while looking at the one-eyed man.

Mitchell's good eye raked from the impassive face to the knife hand and back again.

"And you just listen for a while," Steele told the prisoner. "I'm willing to buy all that old comrade stuff, feller. Because I think you believe it. And because I think you're tough enough to hold out on me. But there was a youngster with you—son of the man who didn't live to ride on Sherrill's last raid? Just nod."

Mitchell nodded.

"So, not an old comrade from the hell-raising jayhawker days." His left hand moved fast, up to his chest to grasp one weighted corner of the scarf. Then it flicked forward. Mitchell tried to step backward. But the free-swinging weighted corner of the scarf curled around the nape of his neck. Steele opened his hand and closed it again. Then he twisted his wrist. There was enough slack in the silken material so that Mitchell was in no danger of choking. But the scarf held his head still when the Virginian rested the knife blade along Mitchell's top lip, one of the honed edges digging into the flesh of the nostrils.

"Just the son of a late friend."

"Mr. Steele!" Joan Ricter pleaded.

"I said shut up, ma'am," Steele reminded, and again he did not take his gaze away from the one big eye of Mitchell. "Maybe you don't owe him so much as the others." He took the knife away from the flesh and spun it toward the ground. It pierced the frost and buried an inch of its blade into the earth beneath. Steele took a weighted corner of the scarf in each hand. "You're going to get a pain in the neck now, feller. Won't kill you. Just put you out. Then we're leaving town. To a place where you can scream your head off and no one can hear you. And you'll scream, feller. Because you won't have a nose, your ears will be gone and you won't be a man anymore. You get the picture? Nod."

Mitchell's single eye blinked several times. He made dry sounds in his throat. Steele tightened the scarf and his prisoner nodded.

The Virginian grunted. "One name and one location. Save yourself a lot of pain. Speak now."

There were more dry sounds in his throat. Then, in a rasping whisper: "It'll be the same. The kid ain't got a tenth the guts his old man had. He'll talk and it'll be the same as if I told you."

Steele nodded, his eyes looking like lifeless, shiny pebbles in the moonlight. "Smell the air, feller. Listen to the night. Look at these two ladies the way a man does. When you wake up things won't ever be the same. But maybe it's worth it for a clear conscience. See you at the hanging."

His hands were crossed over in front of Mitchell's throat. He pushed them further apart, to cut the silk into the sparse flesh.

"Bergen, you bastard!" Mitchell croaked, and continued to speak in a strangled tone even when Steele eased the pressure of the scarf. "Thadius Bergen Junior. The Lazy-R spread, six miles out along the west trail."

Steele released one end of the scarf, with a deft movement of his hand, curled it loosely around his own neck again. "Grateful to you, feller," he said, as he stooped, drew the knife from the earth and replaced it in the holster.

The younger woman vented a low sigh of relief as Steele took the Colt Hartford from her. Her companion snarled.

"Get the other names out of him, Steele!" she demanded. "While you've got him in a talking mood. He's not so tough as he made out he was."

Mitchell was trembling from head to toe, but his thin

lips were compressed tightly together again. Steele glanced at the sadistically excited woman and then looked at the man. The expression of evil intent left his eyes and was replaced by another that was close to respect.

"Even killers have principles, ma'am. I know."

"But he broke!" the woman insisted. "Just from you telling him what you planned to do, he broke!"

"But he didn't welch on a debt," the Virginian reminded. "He doesn't owe Bergen anything."

"But you could have tried!"

"Yeah, I could have tried," Steele allowed, turning to amble toward the arched doorway of the mission.

"Aren't you going to put him on the horse for us?" Joan Ricter asked.

Steele halted and looked back. "Seems one of the Borderville widows still wants to handle things her own way, ma'am. She'll figure something out, I reckon."

"It's because of what happened to Dorrie Sherrill, isn't it?" the blonde asked, her mood of a moment before deflated. "Maybe you're even sorry you took the job now." She shrugged. "All right, if you want to quit, we can't stop you."

"Ignore her, Mr. Steele!" Joan Ricter implored with a glare toward the older woman. "She's talking crazy."

"Yes, ma'am," the Virginian muttered as he moved out through the archway and started across the moon-bright, frost-spread plaza. Only he heard himself add: "And I'm the one that's committed."

CHAPTER SEVEN

Adam Steele understood Wheeler Mitchell's stand so well because he was himself a killer with principles. Not many, but those which had survived the harsh experiences of the violent peace were important to him. And it was one such that caused him to be riding out on the west trail from Carly, his back toward the lightening sky of the breaking dawn.

The principle of seeing a job through to the end, come what may. Whatever feelings he had had toward the Borderville widows—perhaps pity, sympathy and even a sense of affinity—had been slight at the outset. For he had elected to help them because of his good feeling about the town in mourning. True, a town was a barren shell if the people who lived there were discounted. So he had been influenced by the factors he had explained to the blonde he found in O'Ryan's saloon—the lengths to which the widows were prepared to go in achieving their aim.

The affinity had been struck then, because he could recall so vividly the methods he had used to seek revenge against his father's murderers. He could not decide whether pity or sympathy—or both—had been aroused before or after the rapport was established.

Not that it mattered. By his own code, he had to finish the job he had agreed to do. And the fact that he now knew he was hunting down a bunch of killers on behalf of another bunch of killers was immaterial to the depth of his commitment. For he was himself a killer, with no right to judge that others of his kind had not committed their crimes with the same justification he considered he had.

At least, not in this case.

The first shaft of crimson sunlight pierced a bank of cloud in the east and threw his shadow long in front of him as he crested a rise and started down the curving trail toward the Lazy-R spread.

It was a prosperous-looking ranch. There was a low, single-story, L-shaped house with a pitched roof with a barn on one side and a bunkhouse and stable block on the other. Picket fencing enclosed a vegetable garden big enough to supply more produce than the spread would require. The corral was extensive enough to hold fifty horses with room to spare. The whole place was well tended and the woodwork had been given a recent coat of white paint.

It was set in a broad valley which had been well grazed. Cattle—perhaps a thousand head—roamed free and looked in fine condition. There was adequate water for the beef at a lake some two miles south of the ranch buildings.

Smoke wisped from two stacks—one on the house and the other on the bunkhouse. Nobody was outside the buildings.

The trail curved down the side of the valley to bypass a stand of scrub oaks. Steele reined in his mount, slid from the saddle and led the gelding into the timber. Although he was still two hundred yards short of his objective, he could smell the appetizing aromas of brewing coffee and frying bacon on the smoke. The smells worked on the Virginian's gastric juices, but he had to content his hunger with jerked beef and cold beans.

He washed up and shaved, using water from his canteens poured into his hat. The air was warm enough to allow him to remove his top coat after breakfast. He finger-combed his hair and brushed yesterday's trail dust off his suit. He did not feel clean enough, nor stylish enough. But, as with the food, he could be content that he had achieved the best results given the conditions and facilities.

Only briefly did he ponder the fact that his aim in accepting the job offered by the Borderville widows had not been concerned with attaining once more the life of elegance he had enjoyed before the war. As he thought of this, the answer sprang to mind. It was simply that he arrived at Borderville on his way to Mexico. And the past he had sought to revisit south of the border had little to do with a wealthy Virginia dude.

Then he saw Thadius Bergen and devoted his mind entirely to the problem of making the youngster a prisoner.

The fat, acne-scarred kid emerged from the front door of the house, scratching himself and yawning. He was dressed in crisply laundered clothing and highly polished boots. A check shirt and blue denim pants. No gunbelt or hat. He was too far away for Steele to see his expression, but the Virginian sensed an aura of satisfaction about the youngster as Bergen glanced about himself, then strutted across the yard to the bunkhouse.

The hands began to emerge into the yard at the same time. All were taller, broader, harder and older than Bergen. But the kid was the boss and they listened to his orders. A woman in a white dress with a blue apron over it came out on to the house porch and watched. The hands broke from the group, two heading into the barn and the other seven going to the stable.

Bergen returned to the house, interlocked his arm with that of the woman and went from sight.

Steele bided his time in the timber, waiting for the men to emerge from the stable, mount their horses and ride out of the yard. After a while, they separated and

84

headed in different directions, obviously bound for distant areas of the range.

The Virginian swung into the saddle of the gelding then, and completed his ride to the floor of the valley. There was no fence fronting the ranch buildings at the side of the trail and he rode his horse across the yard to the porch. He hitched the reins to a rail before sliding from the saddle.

There was the sound of a hammer hitting metal from the barn. And a man whistling. If those inside the barn or the house had heard the clop of the gelding's hooves, they were not sufficiently interested to check on who was arriving.

Steele slid the Colt Hartford from the boot, turned the handle of the door and pushed it away from him.

". . . father would be proud of you, Thadius," a woman was saying, her tone rich with affection—even adoration. "You know how to handle your inferiors just the way he did."

"He was the finest example any boy could have, Ma," Bergen replied.

China clinked and the sound had an expensive ring to it. There had been the best European porcelain in the diningroom of the plantation house long ago. Its hallway had been twice as large as the one in which Steele now stood, closing the front door behind him and listening to the voices coming through a broad archway on his left.

The Bergens were not so rich as the Steeles had been. But they were far from being paupers and the mother of the killer kept house as cleanly and neatly as had the help around the former Steele residence. The paint on the inside was as fresh and sparkling as that outside. The walls were expensively papered and hung with hand-woven tapestries and fine prints. The furniture was craftsman-made and highly polished. A deep pile carpet was spread across the floor.

It was obvious that, like Wheeler Mitchell, Thadius Bergen had no pressing need for his five thousand share from the Borderville bank money.

As Steele stepped silently over the carpet and halted in the archway, he saw that the living room held further evidence of this fact. But he spent only an instant surveying the surroundings. Then directed his gaze and the Colt Hartford toward the boy and his mother. They were seated on a rococo-style sofa in the center of the large room. In front of them was a low table set with a silver coffee set on a silver salver. The fat youngster and his gray-haired, once-handsome and now aristocratic mother were faced sideways to Steele as they sipped coffee with mannered grace.

"But one thing, dear," Mrs. Bergen said apologetically. "Your father was always willing to show the men he could work as hard and as well as they could."

"I hear the kid did all right at Borderville, ma'am," Steele said, and advanced into the room.

Mother and son snapped their heads around to look at the intruder. The boy saw the rifle, recognized the hard-eyed face, and let the cup and saucer drop from his trembling hands. The fine china hit the edge of the table, shattered and dropped pieces and coffee to the carpet.

"Who are you, sir?" Mrs. Bergen demanded, and was sedate as she lowered her cup and saucer to the table.

"Ma!" Thadius croaked.

As Steele halted in front of him, the Colt Hartford muzzle aimed steadily at the center of his face, the boy reached out a shaking hand. His mother remained in calm anxiety as she accepted it.

"She know about Borderville?" Steele asked.

The coffee smelled good. He felt dirty and ill-used—even clumsily out-of-place—in surroundings he would once have found unsophisticated.

The boy gulped and shook his head.

86

"Borderville?" his mother asked, her confused and fearful gaze switching between her son and Steele. She had a fine complexion and clear eyes, and may have been several years younger than the sixty or so which her white hair indicated.

"No need for her to know, kid," the Virginian offered. "If you come without any fuss."

"The law?" It was a rasping whisper.

"No. But you've got nothing to fear from me—unless you make it difficult."

"There are men in the barn, Thadius," Mrs. Bergen announced, withdrew her hand from that of her son, and stood up. "I'll call them."

Thadius watched his mother make for the window, which was closed. Steele watched the boy, and was able to see the beads of sweat ooze from his wide pores and course over his blotched and scarred face.

"Tell them to bring shovels with them, ma'am," the Virginian said at length. "Any fuss, there'll be a grave to be dug."

"He means it, Ma!"

Mrs. Bergen pulled up short. It was as if she had not quite believed such a thing could be happening in her comfortable home. But she was convinced now, as she turned to show a face as white as her hair.

"Borderville?" she said again, her voice hushed and trembling with emotion. "Did people die? Was there looting? Burning? Raping?"

"Killing and stealing, ma'am," Steele supplied. "Reckon Sherrill's Raiders had their fill of everything else in the jayhawking days."

The old woman—looking closer to seventy now—nodded. "Like father, like son. Sherrill came here, looking for my husband. He was genuinely saddened when I showed him Thadius Senior's grave out back of the house. My husband used to tell our son about the anti-slavery campaign—about what a fine man Clyde Sherrill

87

was." She sighed. "I knew something bad was going to happen when Thadius Junior rode off after Sherrill and was gone for almost a week."

"Ma?" the boy pleaded, his fear heightening as his mother appeared to become resigned to the situation. "Pa would have gone. You admired what Pa did as much as I did. He bought you this spread out of money he got riding with Clyde Sherrill. Clyde needed help and I—"

"On your feet, kid," Steele ordered.

"No! The boy could not help his actions! What he does is born in him!"

She still looked very old, but she moved with a speed of desperation. Her arms were extended in front of her, the fingers curled to form claws. She was aiming for Steele's face.

The Virginian turned toward her, but kept the Colt Hartford trained on Thadius.

"Garrett!" the boy shrieked. "Boyle!"

The woman's scream had a quality almost like that of an Indian war cry.

Steele stepped to the side, seeing that the woman's eyes were tightly closed. She streaked past him. Her son lunged upright and reached across the table, trying to fasten a two-handed grip on her. He almost made it as he stepped forward and kicked over the table, spewing the coffee set and china across the carpet. But the barrel of the rifle slammed against the wrists of the outstretched hands. There was the dry crack of snapping bones and the boy dropped to his knees with a shrill scream of agony.

"Reckon it's not done for Sherrill's Raiders to hide behind their mothers' skirts, kid," the Virginian muttered.

He stepped over the table, fastened a hand over the boy's shirt collar and yanked him upright. His other hand remained fastened around the rifle's frame, finger

88

on the trigger. He jammed the muzzle hard into the small of the quaking back.

Mrs. Bergen realized her blind rush had taken her beyond her objective. She halted, turned and snapped open her eyes.

"Ma, he's got me!" Thadius yelled between sobs. His arms hung loosely at his sides, the wrists already darkening and swelling from the fractures.

The front door of the house crashed open and footfalls sounded heavily on the plush carpet. The two men who pulled up short in the archway were unarmed. Confusion showed in their unintelligent faces.

"Don't do nothin'!" the injured youngster warned. "There's a gun in my back!"

Just for a moment, something close to pleasure injected brightness into the eyes of the two ranch hands.

"Mrs. Bergen?" the one on the left asked.

The charge across the room had drained both energy and hysteria out of the woman. She took two backward steps and sagged against a walnut chest of drawers.

"My son is master of this house," she rasped.

"Back off!" the boy instructed, hissing the words through clenched teeth. "Outside. After we've gone, round up the rest. Come after us."

The two men looked at Steele's nondescriptive handsome face above the fleshy left shoulder of the boy. They were both quizzical and fearful.

"You heard the master's voice, fellers," the Virginian responded. "Not my job to kill him. Intend to see I don't lose him, though."

He started forward, pushing his prisoner ahead of him. Their boots crunched already broken china into smaller pieces. The two hands backed away into the hall.

"Go with them, Ma," the boy rasped. "So I can see you ain't tryin' nothin'. Clyde'll get me outta this. He never lost a man."

Mrs. Bergen tried to comply. She drew herself erect,

anxious eyes boring into the face of her son. She saw agony and terror, smelled his sweat and heard in his voice a confidence she believed to be unfounded. As soon as she lost the support of the chest of drawers, her eyes rolled high in their sockets and she crumpled to the floor.

"Ma!" Thadius called, and made to stoop over her.

The Virginian's grip and the pressure of the rifle muzzle forced him to remain upright. "She'll get over it, kid," Steele growled. "Just couldn't stand the sight of you."

The two hands backed off to the center of the yard.

"You want a horse saddled, Mr. Bergen?" one of them asked.

"I got busted hands, you stupid lunk!" the boy snarled. "How can I ride?"

"Grateful for the offer," Steele added. "But I have an idea I won't have to carry him far."

He leaned his head close to the youngster's ear. "Where's the money, kid?"

"I don't have it. Honest. I give it to Manuel. A weddin' present."

Steele grinned briefly at learning another name. Then he removed the rifle from the base of the boy's spine, swung it high to one side, then whipped it inward again. The barrel slammed into the side of Thad's head, just above his right ear. The boy groaned in expectation of the blow, then became a dead weight, sagging in Steele's single-handed grip.

"Man, I thought the kid was a mean bastard," one of the hands growled scornfully. "But you, you're a son-ofa—"

"Forget it, Garrett," the second man muttered. "Just keep thinkin' about all the crap we took from that little snotnose. Bergen trouble don't have to be our trouble."

Garrett continued to watch Steele with scowling contempt as the Virginian manhandled the unconscious boy

90

across the saddle of the hitched gelding. Then Steele slid the rifle into the boot, unhitched the reins from the porch rail and swung up behind the saddle.

"Just what did the punk kid do to you, mister?" the one named Boyle asked. "For you to give him and his old lady such a hard time."

"I was ready to be polite," Steele replied.

"What'd he do?"

"You wouldn't believe it."

"Try us," Garrett invited.

"Got me a fifty-thousand-dollar job and the pick of a town's women."

Garrett spat.

Boyle said, "If I ever see you again, I'll make sure not to do you any favors, mister."

The Virginian shrugged as he wheeled the gelding and squinted into the bright sun, which had already dispersed the clouds of dawn. "I told you, I was ready to be polite."

Garrett again spat into the dust at his feet. "With a gun in your mitts?"

"Sometimes persuades other people to be polite."

"Didn't work this time though, did it?" Garrett growled, and grinned at the thought he had scored a point against the Virginian.

Steele heeled the gelding into an easy trot across the yard and out on to the trail. "Some you win, some you lose," he muttered, glancing down at the unconscious Bergen slumped over the saddle. Blood had already started to congeal on the rising bruise above the youngster's right ear. "I'm neutral and it's his headache."

CHAPTER EIGHT

"Manuel is the Mexican who rode with Sherrill, that so?" Steele asked Thadius Bergen as the youngster finished making groaning sounds and snapped open his eyes.

After a few moments, the eyes lost their glazed look. They showed pain, then focused upon Steele expressing fear.

"I said Manuel is the Mexican," Steele said.

"Where are we?"

"Stopover. For you on the way to a hanging. For me on the way to a wedding, maybe."

Bergen was sprawled on his back. Only his broken wrists and bruised head complained as he struggled up into a sitting posture. Steele made no comment; just continued to squat on a rock four feet away. Bergen gritted his teeth and looked about him.

They were in a dried-up stream bed between two barren rises. There were boulders and scrub grass. The Virginian's gelding was hobbled close by. The youngster thought he recognized the terrain—some way south of the trail between Carly and the Lazy-R.

"You're with the women?" he asked miserably.

"They're with me," Steele corrected. "Three of them. Followed me out of town, stayed out of sight while I was at the ranch. They're still out of sight, but they're around. Believe me."

Bergen took another hurried look around, with the

same negative result. But then he licked his lips and tasted sweat. The stock of the Colt Hartford seemed to extend a tantalizing promise as it jutted from the boot on the saddle of the gelding.

"Forget it, kid," Steele warned. "It's better than twenty feet to the horse. Maybe I'd let you make it that far. But what does a feller with two broken wrists do with a rifle?"

Bergen groaned, lifted his arms as if to remind himself of his helplessness, and screamed at the sharp pains which seared to his shoulders.

Steele allowed him to recover. But the youngster's painwracked face remained deathly pale, the wanness emphasizing the red and yellow of fresh acne. Then: "Wheeler Mitchell's on his way back to Borderville. He talked. Gave me your name."

Bergen shook his head. "A Sherrill Raider never rats on his buddies."

Steele nodded. And drew the knife from his boot sheath. "He said that and I respected it, kid. But you're just the son of a Sherrill Raider. Convinced him he should give me your name and where I could find you. That's why he's still in one piece. Nothing broken. No pain in the head."

The youngster worked a look of resolution on to his fleshy face. "So frig that one-eyed bastard! You won't get me to talk! I'm my father's son!"

"Your decision, kid," Steele allowed, easing himself wearily to his feet and stepping close to Bergen.

The youngster leaned away from him—too far, and did not have the strength to straighten his back again. He sprawled out in the stream bed.

"Don't kill him, Mr. Steele! He must live to hang!"

The Virginian and the terrified Bergen looked up toward the crest of the east rise. Under the bright orb of the harshly yellow sun, the three women and the four horses were dark silhouettes. But, from their outlines,

93

Steele recognized Amelia Finn, Linda Chambers and Josephine James. It was the maturely handsome Mrs. Finn, with the spare horse on a lead line, who made the request.

A dry sob tremored Bergen's body. His eyes swiveled in their sockets, moving away from the women as they started down the slope, to implore mercy from Steele.

"Can offer you one ray of hope," the Virginian said softly, squatting on his haunches beside the boy. "The one you voiced back home. Sherrill never let one of his men die. Not asking for his location. Just for Manuel's last name and where I can find him."

"Frig off!" Bergen snarled, without convinction. "Pa would never have—"

Steele sighed, slid the knife back into the boot sheath and stood up. "Reckon your pa would have done what he could to protect your ma, kid."

He started toward his horse.

The women came closer.

"Where you . . . what you . . . you better not lay a finger on—"

"Going to the Lazy-R," Steele called back, unfastening the hobble from the gelding's forelegs and swinging up to the mount. "Going to cut her heart out. Then fire the spread. One heart's much like another, so I'll hack off her head. Stick it on a fence pole somewhere close to what's left of the house. So, if Sherrill does spring you, you'll know just what it cost."

The trio of women had reached the stream bed and they looked at the Virginian with much the same degree of horror as Thadius Bergen. Steele's voice as he made the threats was flat and totally lacking in compassion. But his expression of dead-looking eyes and slightly curled back lips added far more weight to his words than the tone in which they were spoken.

"Manuel Gomez!" the kid shrieked. "Ordenos in Sonora! And he'll kill you the second he sees you!"

Steele touched the brim of his hat and his face was suddenly wreathed in a pleasant smile as he glanced at the women. "He won't be any trouble. I had to break his wrists. Means I'll have two of you trailing me to Ordenos, I reckon?"

Linda Chambers, who was a thin-faced redhead of about thirty with the figure of a young boy, looked sick. "Would you have done that?" she rasped.

"No, ma'am."

Bergen vented a dry sob.

"Not under these circumstances," Mrs. Finn said tightly. "But if he wanted something as badly as we want the killers of our menfolk, there isn't anything he wouldn't do."

"No, ma'am," Steele said again, but to a different woman. Then added: "Not anymore. There's nothing I want that badly."

"You want to stay alive, Steele!" Bergen snarled, the veins standing out from the flesh of his throat as he twisted his head to glare at the Virginian. "But there ain't nothin' you can do about that! Not now you crossed up Sherrill's Raiders!"

He choked on the power of his own emotions.

The trio of women had dismounted and, as the boy opened his mouth to yell further threats, Mrs. James kicked dust into it. A coughing fit wracked the boy's frame, then he screamed as the movements erupted new waves of pain along his arms.

The woman, who was a diminutive brunette in her late twenties, turned away from the writhing Bergen and replaced hatred with a wry smile. "Talked up a real dust storm, didn't he?"

Steele remained impassive in response to the smile. "Just hang him, ladies. That was the deal."

Josephine James scowled. "Mite touchy about him, ain't you, Steele? For a man who beat up on him the way you did?"

"Wasn't helpless then, lady," the Virginian rasped. "He is now."

"As were the men folk of Borderville he helped shoot down in cold blood!" Amelia Finn snapped.

"Bringing them in to hang was the deal," Steele insisted in the same even tone. "Getting to be the same as them wasn't."

"But they remain undeserving of sympathy!" the eldest woman snapped. "Best you leave now, if you intend to complete your work."

Steele nodded. "Sure do," he drawled as Thadius Bergen was helped ungently to his feet. The youngster grimaced and succeeded in holding back a cry of agony as his fractured wrists banged against his sides. "And you ladies better be sure of something, too."

"What's that?" the James woman challenged.

"That, apart from being hanged, the kid doesn't have any more bad breaks."

He urged the gelding forward at an easy walk, curving around the group of women and their prisoner, then demanded a gallop. South along the gully and out across a semi-desert. But there were areas of grazing and some of the Lazy-R stock had roamed this far from the verdant valley in which the ranchhouse was sited.

Steele recognized two of the Bergen hands who were engaged in rounding up and herding the strays on this section of the spread. They were far in the distance and they waved when they saw him. The Virginian responded and slowed the gelding to a canter, still heading south.

Once he looked back over his shoulder and saw two riders more than a mile behind him. The hands were hidden behind a low mesa, so it was the women he saw without being able to recognize which of the trio they were.

Over the next four days—the first north of the border and the rest in the foothills of the Sierra Madre of Sonora—he saw them twice more. For the remainder of the time he merely knew they were there, dogging his tracks with remarkable tenacity. Not skill, because, knowing they possessed none, Steele made it simple for them.

If the Borderville widows understood the techniques of a manhunt, they would not have required his assistance. But the will to succeed they had in plenty. Which, in this situation, was all that could be expected of women who had spent their adult lives married to miners and merchants in a small and pleasant town.

Which was why Steele was able to overlook their shortcomings and continue to work for the women, irrespective of the principle which insisted he finish a job he had started. Their shortcomings—the virtual murder of Sherrill's wife and baby and their harsh treatment of prisoners—caused Steele to take a different approach to his job.

The qualities he admired in the women had led him to sow the seeds of a doublecross at the Lazy-R ranch house.

Two American prospectors on widely spaced claims, and the captain in command of a Federal patrol gave him directions to the hillside village of Ordenos. It was a tiny community of dirt farmers, raising cotton and lemons on terraced fields and groves. There was just a single street which climbed the steep slope in a series of humps between the cotton patches and citrus groves. The hovel homes of the farmers and their families were widely spaced. At the top end of the street there was a dual-purpose store and cantina on one side and a church on the other.

It was midafternoon when Steele rode up the street. Peons were at work in the cotton fields. Naked children played around the squalid houses. Burros roamed as freely as dogs.

Nobody paid any attention to the lone American visitor.

The two Borderville widows stayed out of Ordenos, waiting patiently somewhere beyond the final ridge Steele had ridden over to gain his first sight of the village.

Not until the Virginian had dismounted, hitched the gelding to a pole and moved through the open doorway of the cantina was he struck by an obvious thought. He was in Mexico—where he had been headed when he had allowed the massacre of Borderville to alter his plans.

The cantina was pleasantly shady after the bright sunlight he had been riding through all day. But then the inside heat felt higher than that outside. The place smelled of tequila, tobacco smoke, cooking and sweat. In such a cantina, malodorous with the same stinks, in another Mexican village, had he sought to forget the past. And succeeded only in dulling the sharp edge of remorse.

Had he been intent upon returning to Mexico in order to repeat the process?

"Buenas tardes, señor. Haga el favor de sentarse."

The bartender was old and withered. He shuffled out from behind the short length of counter on bare feet and pulled a chair away from a table. He was dressed only in stained and tattered pants. His smile was toothless as he gestured for Steele to be seated.

The place was small enough for six tables, each with two chairs, to make it cramped. There were no other customers.

"Do you have English?" Steele asked, taking the offered seat and resting the Colt Hartford across the table.

"Lo siento mucho," the old man said, and shook his head. Then he waved at flies buzzing across his face. "Sorry, mister. Yes, I speak your language. But we have

few Americans visit us. I forget sometimes. You wish tequila? Beer?"

"I wish to know where I can find Manuel Gomez," Steele replied, ignoring the flies which touched down and launched themselves against his sweaty, tacky skin. There were too many of them for the annoyance ever to be beaten.

The old Mexican clamped his thin lips over his toothless gums. But it merely finished his smile. He was not refusing to talk.

"Manuel is not here, mister. He was here, but now he is gone. I hope you did not come far."

"Far enough, feller. Too far to be satisfied with just that."

The narrow eyes of the old man kept roving to the open doorway and the area of the sun-bright street visible through it.

"A man can say no more than he knows, mister."

The church could be seen through the doorway, on the other side of the street. Steele pointed toward it.

"Did he get married there?"

The old man smiled again. "Ah, you know of Manuel's marriage, mister. You are a friend of his? You know that he is to be joined with Louisa Sorrano."

"Know about his wedding plans," Steele allowed. "They haven't happened yet?"

"A friend would know, I think."

The old man snapped his head around to peer at the archway behind the counter. Steele continued to watch the doorway for a moment longer, until two shadows appeared and the men who cast them showed themselves.

"You will not touch the rifle, *señor*."

Steele looked in the same direction as the old man now. The man who had spoken was one of four who had filed through the archway and aligned themselves behind the counter. Like the two blocking the doorway, they leveled guns at Steele. Two old Navy Colts, a Henry repeater and three Springfields.

The men had come in from the fields, still wearing their cotton pants and shirts, their sombreros, and the sweat and grime of toil.

"You will tell us the reason you seek Manuel Gomez."

The old man who ran the cantina shuffled off to the most distant corner and spoke fast in his native tongue. His fellow villagers listened with no show of emotion. They were all younger than the man delivering the report. But none was young. They looked underfed, overworked and hopelessly resigned to their lot in life.

"He says he has told you nothing, *señor*," the spokesman for the peons translated. "It is unnecessary. Manuel Gomez is the most respected citizen of Ordenos. Each of us knows that no other man, woman or child in this place would betray Manuel. Your reason, *señor*?"

Steele jutted out his lower lip to direct a stream of air against his nose. A fly buzzed angrily away, then settled on his forehead. "The reception committee maybe means you already know, feller."

Neither of the men in the doorway understood English. Two of those behind the counter were also perplexed by the exchange.

"We are simple farmers, *señor*. We do not invite trouble for we have to struggle much to do no more than feed ourselves and our families. Manuel told us an Americano might come in search of him. You are the man he described."

Steele nodded, recalling how he had been scrutinized by the Sherrill bunch on the trail outside Borderville. "Did he say what you were to do about it, feller?"

"Manuel has given much to this village. Many years ago, after the wars which your Americans fought against each other, he returned to his birthplace. He was rich, but he shared what he had and soon he was

100

poor again. For money does not make money in a village such as Ordenos. Then he went away again. Not for long. And returned, a rich man once more. We refused to accept a share of his wealth, señor. We told him to take his betrothed and to make a good life for himself in a better place than this. When he told us you might come, even then we refused payment."

"Payment for what, feller?"

"Not to kill you, señor. We are farmers, not *pistoleros*. But we will protect what is ours in any manner we have to. Manuel is ours. Owed much by us.

"Yes, we know the reason you came." He shook his head. "Enough of it, anyway, señor. Why you want Manuel does not matter. Perhaps it is better we do not know."

One of the men in the doorway spat out some angry-sounding Spanish. The spokesman for the group nodded vigorously. The others matched the gesture.

"I have talked much, señor. And I am reminded that we promised Manuel that we would hold our silence. He did not ask this, you understand. He warned us only that you would be coming. We promised his silence. You will leave now, señor. If you do not, or if you return ever, we will kill you. Not as *pistoleros* kill. As simple farmers protecting what is ours."

"Grateful for the choice," the Virginian said evenly, as hooves clopped on the street of Ordenos. He reached out a gloved hand and fisted it around the extreme end of the Colt Hartford's barrel. There were grunts and the motley selection of weapons were thrust toward him threateningly. "Different things are important to different people. You fellers have your farms. I have this rifle."

He stood up and canted the Colt Hartford to his left shoulder—upside down. Without waiting for an answer, he turned his back on the men behind the counter and moved toward the doorway. The men guarding it held their ground, the aim of their Colts wavering as they directed nervous glances toward the spokesman.

Behind them, Amelia Finn and Linda Chambers reined in their horses, wheeling them to face the cantina. They leaned forward, trying to peer into the deeply shaded interior.

"Mr. Steele?" Mrs. Finn called, a little anxiously.

"You have helpers, *señor*? Women?"

Steele halted in front of the guards on the door. "Widows," he replied without turning around. "Of men Gomez killed. There are a lot more—"

"I said it is better we do not know what Manuel has done!" the Mexican cut in sharply.

"Mr. Steele!" Mrs. Finn called again, louder. "We saw the men come in from the fields and get guns. Are you—"

The spokesman said a single word in his native tongue. The woman curtailed her inquiry as the two Mexicans in the doorway stepped aside.

At no time since entering the cantina had Steele showed himself to be anything but relaxed. Initially, he had not trusted the gunmen and fear had contributed to the tautness behind his surface nonchalance. But even after he was convinced that they preferred not to harm him, he remained poised to take advantage of an opening.

The opportunity came now.

As the two men in front of him stepped back, he lunged at them.

"Beat it!" he roared at the women.

He whipped the rifle down from his shoulder and tilted it to the side, swinging up his free hand to accept the stock. The Colt Hartford was now a bar held across his chest. He lowered his right hand to make allowance for the difference in the men's heights.

The women were held immobile by surprise for a moment. Then they saw the flurry of activity in the

102

doorway and heard cries of alarm. They wheeled their mounts and raced back down the steep slopes of the street.

The stock of the rifle crashed into the jaw of one Mexican. The end of the barrel hit the cheek of the other, the foresight gouging out a bloody rut.

Both went down hard to the floor, the tone of their cries altering from alarm to pain. Expectation of bullets driving into his flesh caused sweat to squeeze from every pore in the Virginian's back. But he had called it right. Once he accepted that the Mexicans truly were simple farmers not relishing the need to carry guns, he had to believe they would take time to think before using the weapons.

And the amount of time they took enabled him to power between the fallen men, go over the threshold and swing to the right.

Behind him Mexican voices were raised, the words spat out in the tone of curses. A single shot exploded, the bullet cracking through the doorway to thud into the adobe front of the church across the street.

Steele flattened himself against the wall of the cantina and glanced along the street. The two women were galloping their horses at full speed. Behind them, nothing moved except the dust spurted up by the racing hooves.

The playing children were gone. The door of every adobe hovel was closed.

Inside the cantina, the cursing was ended by the shouted order of the man in charge. Then boot leather scraped the hard-packed dirt of the floor. Voices sounded again, as hissed whispers.

Steele crouched to go under the glassless window, then straightened to move around the corner to the side wall of the cantina. There were some casks there and he used them to climb up onto the roof. From this vantage point he could see the entire town and the terracing on

103

either side. Mrs. Finn and Linda Chambers were beyond the final houses and still heeling their mounts at a flat-out gallop across the open country.

If frightened eyes were watching him from the houses and lemon groves, Steele could not sense them. Certainly, no warnings were shouted that he was on the cantina roof. He went to the rear and spread himself full length. The sun-heated adobe burned him through his vest and shirt and pants.

There was total silence below him for some long seconds. Then a door creaked as it was cracked open. It creaked again when it was eased wide. A sombrero-shaded head was stuck out. A word whispered and the man emerged, head moving from side to side to rake his eyes toward every hiding place; but only at ground level. He beckoned with a hand and another man came out. One of them had the Henry and the other a Springfield.

The second man did look up, but the movement of his sombrero telegraphed the intention and Steele was able to draw himself into the cover of the roofline. He heard their boots against the ground as they split up, to explore both sides of the cantina.

As soon as the back lot was clear, he turned around, swung his legs off the roof and lowered himself to the ground, one-handed. His other hand remained fisted around the frame of the rifle, finger curled against the trigger.

The rear door was still open. Steele went through it, gripping the Colt Hartford two-handed now.

The fetid air of the kitchen was almost nauseating. A rat scuttled from a burst-open sack of flour for the cover of an undraped latrine hole. Steele reached the archway to the public area in four silent strides.

There were no men behind the counter anymore. The two scouts reached the street, exchanged whispers and called in through the windows. Men moved out of cover to go to the door. Steele waited until they had filed ten-tatively out through doorway, then emerged from the archway.

The toothless owner of the place, stripped to the waist, was still against the wall where he had retreated from the threat of crossfire. He saw the Virginian and his mouth gaped open. Just a tiny sound trickled over his trembling lower lip.

Steele raised an extended finger to his own compressed lips. The Mexican crossed himself, put his hands together and mouthed a silent prayer toward the smoke-blackened ceiling.

The Mexicans with guns had gathered in the center of the street. They were in a close group, listening to something the top man was saying. Steele went around the end of the counter, circled the tables and chairs, and showed himself in the doorway. The stock of the rifle was against his shoulder and his left eye was behind the backsight.

He fired, cocked the hammer, fired, cocked the hammer. Five times the revolving rifle exploded, the shots carefully placed by a marksman who made no attempt to retreat into cover.

There sombreros were scaled off heads. And two pairs of booted feet were sprayed with dust by bullets thudding into the ground.

There were shrieks of alarm and a flurry of movement. Three men made to retreat; the other three held their ground but swung their guns to the aim. A Colt in the hands of the man with a split cheek. And two Springfields.

"Hold it!" Steele snarled.

Those who had started to flee were abruptly halted. The two rifles and the revolver drew beads on the Virginian, but fingers were stayed against the triggers. Shock and fear was evenly distributed among the Mexicans.

"Five of you could be dead!" Steele said, moderating his tone.

"Your rifle, it holds six bullets?" This from the spokesman for the group, re-establishing his position. It was he who aimed the Springfield.

"One left, feller. If I die, I take one of you with me."

A nod. "I recognize the danger, *señor*. I also recognize that five of us could be dead, had you wished it. It is not hard for a *pistolero* to trick simple farmers. But you are no ordinary *pistolero*, I think."

"I don't know what I am," the Virginian answered. "But I know what I want."

"Manuel Gomez."

Only the Mexican doing the talking continued to concentrate his eyes and his aim on Steele. The others switched their attention back and forth.

"And some others, feller. But we're only concerned with Gomez right now."

"I would rather die than betray a man who has—"

"Killed every man in a town much bigger than Ordenos," Steele cut in. "With the help of nine others who are due to hang for the same crime."

The other Mexican who understood English was startled by the revelation. He was asked a question in his native tongue and, as Steele slowly recounted the details of the Borderville massacre, those who did not understand directly were given a translation. Fear was driven from their faces, as horror became etched into the dark flesh.

When the story was told, only a Springfield was aimed at Steele. The man holding it remained as impassive as the man telling the story.

Then: "*Señor,* I said it was better we did not know what Manuel had done. Always in Ordenos he has been a good, kind, gentleman. But there are those who live here who chose to believe Manuel could not get rich so quickly by being the man he was in our town."

106

"Reckoned there were more than six guns in this town," Steele drawled, and lowered the Colt Hartford as the Springfield was tilted from the aim.

The Mexican nodded, his expression melancholy. "Just this time, you understand. Before, he was away so long, there was no suspicion. But this time, so much for so little time away from Ordenos. There was much suspicion. More even, when Manuel said you might come for him. We did not share in his good fortune, *señor*. But we . . ." He waved a hand to encompass the immediate group, ". . . still felt we owed a debt for the first time."

The translator was keeping the others informed of the exchange. A man interrupted to speak fast Spanish. All the others nodded.

"He says we did not dream that Manuel was capable of such a crime, *señor*. But it is not only for this I tell you what you wish to know. I tell it because you showed you are willing to die if you fail. And in dying would have taken just a single life in payment for your own. This, though you could have—"

"You got my point, feller," Steele cut in. "I know why I made it."

"A place called Millertown, north of the border," the spokesman supplied. "Manuel was to have been married here in our church. But he has friends in this place called Millertown. I think, perhaps, he recognized that he had no friends here where he was born. Just people who are in his debt."

"Grateful to you," the Virginian acknowledged, and moved to his horse. He slid the Colt Hartford into the boot, unhitched the reins and swung up into the saddle. He glanced from the top of the street to the crest of the next hill north and saw the two women waiting there.

The cantina owner came out of his premises, holding up a bottle of tequila. "Here, mister! On behalf of the wives of Ordenos who are not widows."

107

Steele shook his head as he jerked on the reins to wheel the gelding away from the cantina. "I tried that once before in Mexico, feller."

The toothless man shrugged and lowered the bottle as, all along the street, the doors of the hovels were opened and smiling men and women emerged. The men who had sought to protect Manuel Gomez were still shocked and saddened by having their suspicions about him confirmed.

"Perhaps you made a wise decision, mister," the cantina owner growled, and grimaced at the label on the bottle. "Manuel was the only rich man Ordenos had. So I stock only the cheapest liquor. It would have been a poor reward for what you have done."

Steele touched the brim of his hat as he heeled the gelding forward. "I try to do things only for the best, feller."

CHAPTER NINE

In one respect only had it been that way since the start of the violent peace. Steele wanted the best for himself and his actions were invariably directed toward achieving that end, irrespective of the effect upon other people.

But, since he began to work for the Borderville widows, his attitude had changed. And his thought processes and physical responses to them were similar to those of the war. The cause was the town without men and the plan of campaign had been devised by the women who were left. The enemy was the Sherrill bunch.

Steele was a soldier again—albeit of fortune. And he was applying the rules to which he had adhered in the war of long ago. Recognizing that there were faults on both sides, he was committed to helping one against the other. To make this position tenable to himself he had to fight with honor.

Thus, he would kill without compunction if his survival was at stake, but would always do what was in the best interests of the enemy and the innocent bystanders if such an alternative was available.

The Virginian found this distinctly odd as he rode north once more. There had been no village like Ordenos on the battleground of the East. Perhaps there had been farms and homesteads similar to the Lazy-R. Maybe places like Carly. Certainly no terrain that bore any resemblance to the Sierra Madre of Sonora or the rock hills and scrub deserts of southern Arizona.

The people? They were much the same wherever a man traveled.

So, it was entirely in his mind—the sense that he had been here before and was doing exactly the same thing for the second time in his life.

The women were out of sight before Ordenos was hidden by the foothills. But he knew they were close by, physically trailing him toward the scene of the next skirmish in his strange one-man war against a scattered enemy.

Just the memory of what had happened in the Mexican village stayed with him. Alongside the recollections of the incidents at the Lazy-R and at Carly. All of these adding up to the awareness that nothing he had done since Borderville was for his own good.

"So maybe you're just a nice feller," he said aloud, and the gelding's ears pricked up. He grinned, not realizing he had spoken aloud. Then: "Sure, I'm a nice feller. Kind to old ladies, horses and dogs."

The gelding snorted and it had a contemptuous tone in the hot emptiness of the lonely late afternoon. Steele stroked the animal's neck with a gloved hand.

"It'll pass," he said softly. "All good things have to come to an end."

Five days later, with his supplies almost exhausted, Steele rode into Millertown. It was north and far to the east of Borderville, on the stage trail linking Tucson with Tombstone. The stage depot was the center point of the town and, from the barrenness of the surrounding country, seemed the sole and unlikely purpose of the community's existence. But there was also a law office, three stores, a church, two saloons, a hotel, a restaurant, a livery stable, a blacksmith and a row of identical houses. All the construction was along the east side of the single street, which was just a section of the trail.

110

Apart from the stage depot and the houses which were solid frame, the town was jerry-built, with once impressive false fronts concealing the ugliness of hurried and cheap construction. But, whatever dream Millertown had been built on had failed to become a reality. The houses and the false fronts of the commercial buildings had weathered and been neglected. Paint was faded and peeling and timbers were cracked.

It was night when Steele reached the town and just a few windows showed gleams of lamplight to compete with the moon and stars. Many of the buildings which were in darkness emanated an air of being abandoned. Just two chimneys gave off woodsmoke—indicating that the law office and one of the saloons were the only places heated against the bitter cold of the night. These were also the only buildings showing lights.

There was nobody on the street.

Steele did not trust the rotted timber of the hitching rail outside the saloon and tied the gelding to a post supporting the porch canopy. As he glanced around, he saw the two women astride their horses a half mile out in open country.

He slid the Colt Hartford from its boot and entered the saloon, having to open double doors before he pushed through the swing doors.

It was a big place, single-story, long and low. Cold, except for a small area around the only stove which was lit. The two men who sat in front of the stove looked at the newcomer with a total lack of enthusiasm.

"You want a drink?" one of them asked.

"Just don't get drunk," the other added.

Both spoke in the manner of men with no interest in the response they drew.

Steele moved across a floor spread with old sawdust, weaving between tables and chairs layered thickly with ancient dust. The counter along the back of the saloon was also neglected for most of its considerable length.

The five other stoves evenly spaced around the room might never have been lit. The few ceiling lamps there were shed only a partial light—their glass covers encrusted with grime.

"Coffee on your bill of fare?" the Virginian asked.

"Restaurant don't serve hard liquor and I don't try for any of their action." This man was tall and thin and about fifty. His hands and face were clean but his shirt and pants and the leather apron he wore on top were all as filthy as his surroundings. The lines inscribed into his pale skin seemed to have been formed by countless years of showing no other expression but a scowl.

"Restaurant only opens when a stage comes through. Northbound scheduled for nine tomorrow mornin'." This man wore the badge of sheriff pinned to his long top coat. He was short and stocky, with the face of a sixty year old. It was a sun-bronzed face, decorated with a gray moustache and bushy eyebrows of the same color. He wore a ten-gallon hat, pushed back over a head of thinning gray hair. His coat was buttoned from throat to knee, tight-fitting enough to contour a holstered revolver.

"A man has to take the rough with the smooth," Steele acknowledged. "Any objection if I share the warmth? Seeing as how the stove is lit?"

The bartender and the sheriff had turned chairs away from a nearby table to face the stove. Each held an almost full glass of beer. The drinks had lost their heads and looked flat.

"Ain't no law against that, son," the sheriff muttered.

"Welcome, until I close up the place," the bartender added. "Passin' through?"

Steele turned a chair for himself and sat down, resting the rifle across his thighs as he extended his gloved hands toward the source of the heat, "Hope to," he replied.

"Ain't nobody does anythin' else, son," the lawman

112

said mournfully. "Millertown ain't got nothin' for nobody to stay for. Not since old Job Miller's idea for makin' the desert bloom didn't pan out."

He laughed at a private joke. It was a bad joke and the harshness of his laughter explained how bad. The bartender continued to look sour.

"If I can find somebody to point me in the right direction," Steele added.

"From Millertown, any direction is the right one," the bartender growled.

"Which way do you want to go, son?"

"The same way Manuel Gomez went."

The name captured the attention of the two locals. Both lost interest in infinity, sipped at their beers, and looked at Steele.

"At the hotel with his new bride," the bartender said.

"Damn you, Saul," the sheriff said without any trace of venom in his tone or expression. "You always were too fast with your mouth." He continued to keep his dull eyes directed toward Steele. "You bringin' trouble to Millertown, son?"

"Reckon to take it away with me, Sheriff."

The old lawman shook his head. "Millertown's dyin', son. But it ain't dead yet. And I figure to keep it lawful and orderly long as it or me stays alive."

He started to unbutton his coat. Saul resumed his interest in a distant corner of the grubby saloon.

"Don't know much about this Manuel Gomez or his new wife, son. Except they came to be married in our church."

He had opened his coat all the way, and now he draped a knarled left hand over the butt of his holstered Navy Colt. Steele's gloved hands continued to rest easily on the rifle, which was uncocked and aimed a foot to the right of the lawman.

"Special reason for holding the wedding here?" the Virginian asked conversationally.

113

A slow nod. "He's got friends here, son. Charlie Pike, who runs the restaurant and Matt Webb, our blacksmith."

Steele showed no visible reaction to the tautness of excitement that gripped him. "Buddies from the war?"

"What I hear, son. Held the weddin' breakfast in Charlie's place. Lots of hard liquor served there today. But took out from here. Men got drunk and talked about the war. Some drunk enough to disturb the peace. Charlie and Matt are in my cells now, son. Be let out come mornin'."

"You're slower, Morgan," the bartender growled. "But you say a lot more than me."

The sheriff sighed, still maintaining his steady scrutiny of Steele. "This man come to Millertown lookin' for information about another man, Saul. Maybe he's lookin' for trouble, too. More or less said he was lookin' for trouble, didn't he? Figure to be civil to him. So maybe he'll take his trouble someplace else."

"You have any ideas, Sheriff?" the Virginian asked.

Another sigh. "Only ever had one idea in my life, son. That was to throw in my lot with old Job Miller. Turned out to be one hell of a lousy idea. So I don't have them no more. Figure a man can only be sure of the facts. One fact is that Manuel Gomez and his bride'll be leavin' on the northbound stage at nine o'clock tomorrow. Another fact is that my jurisdiction ends at the town marker."

The lawman got some emotion into his eyes now. They expressed a plea.

The bartender backed him up with words. "Charlie and Matt are the first men Morgan's arrested in five years, stranger. And he only managed that on account of they were dead drunk and ready to lay their heads down anyplace. Cells were as good as any."

"Any other reason?" Steele asked the sheriff. "For making it easy for me?"

114

Morgan sniffed. "The Mexican was through here a while back, son. With a couple of other fellers. Charlie and Matt downed tools and rode out with them. They came back the same as they left. But the Mexican, he wasn't no peon no more. Dressed like some fancy don. And the woman he was fixin' to marry, she had on every kinda finery a man can imagine."

"Morgan's always had somethin' about folk that get rich quick," the bartender said, and sipped his beer. "Ever since old Job Miller held out that promise to us and some others. Only for us and the others, it never worked out."

The sheriff ignored him. "Course, son, that Gomez might have good reason. And you, you might be the most evil feller ever set foot on earth. But it ain't none of my business if scores are settled outside my jurisdiction."

"Steele nodded and got to his feet, canting the Colt Hartford to his shoulder. The sheriff grunted and put down his glass so that he could refasten his coat.

"Northbound, due to leave at nine?"

"Right, son."

"Something else," Steele said.

"Yeah, son."

"Whose peace did the drunks disturb?"

The bartender held up a hand, the fingers and thumb splayed. "Feller who runs the stage depot, the preacher, owner of the hotel, Morgan here, and me."

"All that's left," the sheriff explained. "Plus Charlie and Matt, of course. They might give you trouble. Seem to be real big buddies of the Mexican."

"Grateful for the information," the Virginian replied, and raised a hand in farewell before he turned to wend his way between the tables and chairs to the door.

"He do somethin' bad to get so rich so quick, son?" Morgan called.

115

"Pretty bad," Steele answered. "He's wanted by some people who reckon to hang him."

"Obliged, son. That'll keep my conscience clear."

"Know how you feel, feller," the Virginian muttered as he swung wide the double doors and closed the meager warmth in the saloon again.

The women were still out where he had seen them when he arrived. But they had dismounted now.

He unhitched the gelding, swung up into the saddle and rode along the street, past the three empty stores, the church, the restaurant, the abandoned second saloon and halted outside the lit window of the law office. He had never booted the rifle and it was still in his left hand as he slid from the saddle and cracked his right palm against the flank of the horse.

The animal snorted and lunged into a gallop—raising dust out along the trail that stretched toward Tucson. He watched the horse until it slowed, veered off the trail and started to crop on a patch of scrub grass. As far as he was able to tell, only he and the two women had seen what happened.

He went into the law office now. It was much smaller than the saloon and the single stove kept it pleasantly warm. It was a rectangular room with timber walls. The rear portion was partitioned off into two cells by iron bars. A man lay sprawled on a cot in each of them. Both were snoring loudly. One had been sick and the stink of his vomit was still strong.

There was a single key hanging from a nail in the end of an empty rifle rack. It fitted both locks and turned them with a screech of unoiled mechanism. The hinges of the doors creaked.

Neither of the inmates were disturbed by the sounds. Both of them were in their mid-thirties. The callused hands of the one with long, ink-black hair indicated that he was Matthew Webb, the town's blacksmith. The man

116

who ran the restaurant was shorter and thinner and had blond hair. It was he who had been sick.

Both were dressed in city suits, polished boots and neckties. They had flowers in their buttonholes.

Steele used the Colt Hartford as a lever to tip Pike onto the floor. The man grunted, but then sank back into his drunken stupor as the Virginian dragged him out of the cell and into the office. When Steele used the same technique on Webb, the blacksmith snapped open his eyes and cursed.

"You're disturbing the peace again, feller," the Virginian muttered, and swung the rifle stock against the top of Webb's head.

He found a lariat on a hook behind the lawman's desk, cut off a length of rope and used it to bind the men's wrists together, above their heads. Then he tied both pairs of wrists in a single loop and draped the free end over his shoulder. He dragged the men across the floor of the office and out onto the street. As he closed the door behind him, the women mounted and began to ride toward town. But they reined in their horses when Steele held up a hand.

After the warmth of the saloon and the law office, the night felt colder than before. But Steele was sweating with exertion before he had covered half the distance to where the women waited. He rested often, wiping sweat from his forehead as he glanced back to where the meager lights of Millertown continued to gleam against the dark façades of the saloon and law office.

"Two?" Amelia Finn said, her tone one of grim satisfaction.

"Neither of them the Mexican!" Linda Chambers stated, after darting forward to squat and look closely at the faces of the prisoners. "He's not here?"

Steele sucked in deep breaths, as he untied the drag

117

rope and then used his knife to cut it into two equal lengths.

"For sure he's here," he replied, thrusting the ropes toward Mrs. Finn. "I can't be so certain these two were at Borderville."

"Then why—?"

"Just ninety-five percent sure, ma'am. Tie them up load them up and take them home with you."

"But what if—"

"Best you treat them kindly, ladies. In the event I have to apologize to them."

"The Mexican?" the younger woman asked.

"I'll make sure he gets to Borderville," the Virginian assured.

"The others? Shall we send women to collect them?"

"I'll take care of delivery."

Both women started to ask more questions, but Steele turned his back on them and moved off on a diagonal course from the one he had taken away from town.

The gelding waited patiently for him, and showed no rancor for the blow that had caused his bolt. Steele rode him slowly and easily back along the trail and onto the street. The women had done as he instructed and ridden out of sight with the unconscious men slumped over their horses. But he sensed they were waiting in cover, watching him.

Steele halted his horse across from the hotel, on the opposite side of the street. He drew the Colt Hartford from the boot, cocked it as he swung it one-handed to aim at the night sky, and squeezed the trigger.

"Gomez!" he called. "Manuel Gomez!"

Men shouted. In the hotel, the saloon still in business and the stage depot. A woman screamed in the hotel

"Who wants me? Who is it calls the name of Manuel Gomez?" The questions had been prefaced by the screech of timber on timber as a second-story window of the hotel was slid open.

118

Further down the street the double doors of the saloon crashed back and a wedge of light stabbed out to augment the moon glow.

Speaking on behalf of four other men!" Steele answered, the rifle lowered and resting across the saddlehorn. "Mitchell from Carly! Bergen from the Lazy-R! Pike and Webb from Millertown! They need help!"

The Mexican showed himself at the window. His white night-shirt was a blur of lighter color against the dark of the room and hotel façade. A woman was speaking anxiously to him in fast Spanish.

"Son!" the town sheriff called. "I told you, son! No trouble in my town!"

He had stepped out into the wedge of light from the open doorway. His coat was unbuttoned and his Navy Colt was drawn.

He fired and his bullet exploded a divot of dirt midway between the saloon and where Steele sat on the gelding.

"Help?" Gomez demanded.

The sheriff started to run, and fired again.

"You're a crazy old fool, Morgan!" the bartender snarled from the safety of the saloon.

The second shot from the revolver went high over Steele's head. The Virginian sighed, and threw the Colt Hartford up to his shoulder. The sheriff's gun spat a bullet and muzzle flash. The bullet cracked a lot closer to Steele this time. But it was the last one the handgun would ever fire. The shell from the rifle smashed into the cylinder of the revolver and sent the weapon spinning out of the lawman's grasp. The man yelled and pulled up short, wringing his bruised hand.

"Disturbing the peace, feller!" Steele told him as other doors and windows were slammed open. "You shouldn't try to shoot a man for that!"

"You said you got Charlie and Matt!" the sheriff snarled. "That's jail-breakin'!"

119

"You freeze, *señor!*" Gomez ordered from the window. "I have you covered!"

Steele was as certain as ever that the Mexican would not use a gun until his anxious curiosity had been satisfied. So he continued to aim his gaze and the rifle toward the lawman. "You're right, feller. But I didn't do them any favor."

"*Señor!*" Gomez bellowed, cutting across another burst of Spanish from his bride.

Steele turned only his head toward the window now, his hat brim still keeping his face in deep moon shadow. "We'll talk if you want to," he called. "In Borderville!"

He slammed his heels into the flanks of the gelding and, for the second time that cold night, the animal snorted a protest as a forward lunge was commanded.

A revolver cracked a bullet through the open window of the hotel. It went wide, aimed by a surprised man at a moving target. Steele raked the gun around and elevated it, crashing two shots in the approximate direction of the window. The lead thudded into the false front of the hotel. Steele slid the rifle into the boot, took up the reins and jerked them over to send the gelding into a curving turn.

More revolver shots were aimed at him, but he was crouched low in the saddle, urging the horse into ever-increasing speed. Bullets cracked over his head and around his body, digging harmlessly into the ground.

Shouts from the two Mexicans and from a handful of Millertown citizens counter-pointed the gunshots. Then the revolver rattled empty and the hoofbeats of the galloping gelding masked the voices. Steele came erect in the saddle and soon was out of earshot. But he did not ease the horse back to a steady trot until he was out of effective rifle range.

"You idiot!" Linda Chambers accused a few minutes later, as she and Mrs. Finn emerged from around a rock

120

outcrop. "Did you think he would just surrender to you?"

Both women were mounted. Their prisoners were securely strapped to the horses, their ankles lashed together and linked by a rope to their wrists under the bellies of the animals. The men were still unconscious, one from drinking and the other from the crack on his head.

"No, ma'am," the Virginian answered without reining in his horse. "But unless he was willing to talk, Millertown was a dead end."

He rode on beyond them and they urged their horses after him.

"He'd have talked!" the younger woman rasped. "We'd have made him, if you're too weak in the stomach to do what's necessary."

"You're getting close to the part that's troubling me, ma'am," the Virginian muttered. "What with you women and all this riding."

"Close? What is that supposed to mean?"

Steele moved into a more comfortable posture on the saddle. "Getting to be a real pain in the ass, ladies."

CHAPTER TEN

Borderville no longer smelled of old death; but the threat of future dying hung over the town. It was plain for all to see, taking the form of ten gallows erected on the crest of the hill to the south.

Steele, the two widows and their two prisoners saw the gallows from a great distance, in the clear light of early morning. There were five horses in the group now, Pike and Webb having a mount each purchased from the expenses money the widows had given the Virginian.

Although they were still securely bound, the mood of the prisoners had improved since they were made more comfortable. Previously sour and taciturn, except to growl obscenities at their captors, both men became talkative. Initially, they boasted of their part in the massacre and were full of confidence that Sherrill would ensure they did not hang.

Then, in face of the women's grim resolution that they would, and Steele's total lack of response, they sought to justify what had happened at Borderville, adopting a line similar to that which Wheeler Mitchell and Thadius Bergen had taken. They owed Clyde Sherrill a favor for the many he had done them during the jayhawking days . . . Sherrill had good reason for raiding Borderville, since the town attempted to hang him unjustly and when it couldn't, killed his wife and child . . . the money stolen from the bank was not to be put to selfish use; would rather have been invested in Millertown for the good of all who still believed in the dream of its founder.

Their arguments were ignored and they reverted to blustering confidence again—until they saw the gallows. They were abruptly silent then, and the sweat of fear sheened their faces in sunlight too fresh to be warm.

"The money!" Linda Chambers said suddenly as the group started down the final half mile of trail toward town. "You didn't recover the shares of these two!"

The sun was clear of the horizon and hot by then. Steele glanced over his shoulder. The women were dirty and weary, the men dirty, unshaven but well-rested. Having posed the point, the younger widow appeared as indifferent to the Virginian's response as her companion and the prisoners.

"Way I understand it, ma'am, it was my money. A man can do what he likes with his own money."

There was not even a nod of acknowledgment and Steele faced front again.

The widows who had stayed in Borderville had not confined their energies to building the gallows. They had done their own traditional chores and the work of their menfolk. Thus, the town was neat and tidy, this impression drawn from more than mere polished windows and swept stoops. The bank had been repaired, the funeral parlor wreckage had been cleared and construction was underway on another building to occupy the same lot, and every trace of the massacre had been eradicated from the meeting point of the streets in front of the church.

Every commercial establishment was open for business and out in the hills at the western extreme of Mine Road there were signs of activity to indicate that the silver mines were being worked.

As the five riders entered town, Steele's sense of being carefully watched was proved to be true. The bell

123

in the stunted tower of the church clanged three times. Within moments, Main Street's sidewalks were suddenly crowded with women and children. And the activity in the hills abruptly quickened in pace, as wagons were abandoned and saddled horses were mounted.

A dry sob exploded from Pike's lips.

"Clyde'll spring us, frig it!" Matt Webb snarled.

"It's Steele!" the young and pretty Julia King shouted. "With only two of them!"

She lunged out of the doorway of the schoolhouse and sprinted down the street ahead of the riders, holding up the skirts of her dress. "Mrs. Salisbury, it's Mr. Steele coming back!"

"I see him, Julia!" Margery Salisbury replied grimly, moving down off the sidewalk in front of the drugstore.

She waited in the center of the street, fists clenched on her slim hips, eyes shining in the bright sunlight and mouth firmly closed. The young girl went to the opposite sidewalk. The rest of the women in town watched in silence. Those who had been at the mine workings were galloping their horses toward town, most of them lost to sight in billowing dust.

"Amelia . . . Linda," Mrs. Salisbury greeted as Steele reined in his gelding and touched the brim of his hat. "Take the prisoners to join the others in the cells of the courthouse. Then rest up."

She returned her attention to the Virginian, as the women from the silver mines skidded their horses to a dust-raising halt in front of the church. "You'll be leavin' directly, I hope?"

"No, ma'am."

"He says he has a plan, Margery," Mrs. Chambers muttered.

"I'm quite aware of one of his plans," the widow of the town druggist snapped.

She was wearing a capacious apron over her dress. As soon as Steele had halted his horse, she had removed

124

her hands from her hips to delve them into the front pocket of the apron. Now she withdrew both of them, and aimed a Frontier Colt at the Virginian's chest.

Steele experienced icy fear as a tight ball in the pit of his stomach, for he had expected nothing greater than anger from the woman. On each side of the street, women leaned into open doorways and withdrew a wide variety of weapons. Rifles and revolvers. The riders in front of the church slid rifles from their saddle-hung boots and urged their horses into a slow advance.

"Well, what d'you know?" Matt Webb growled.

"It don't help us," Charlie Pike pointed out miserably.

"Margery?" Mrs. Finn asked shrilly.

"You'll be shot down, Steele!" the handsome widow of the druggist warned. "Or you may surrender. In that event, you will be held until after the hangin's and then released."

"Same as the two marshals you fixed to come here, mister!" the sour-faced Amy Richards snarled from the doorway of the Far West Saloon.

Steele pursed his lips and sighed. Claire Johnston, a Remington revolver held firmly in her right hand, advanced from the livery stable. "Bergen's mother managed to get two lawmen?"

The fleshy, faintly Latin-looking woman with the Remington halted beside his horse. She delved a hand into the split of his pants leg to take the knife first. Then reached up to slide the Colt Hartford from the boot. As he saw the rifle taken, Steele experienced anger take over from fear. It was a logical progression, for he believed he had nothing to fear from the Borderville widows, provided he complied with their demands. And there was nothing else he could do, without sacrificing his life.

"Take good care of that rifle, ma'am," he warned softly.

125

"So you're not goin' to deny you doublecrossed us?" Mrs. Salisbury snapped, as Claire Johnston retreated to the livery stable with the knife and Colt Hartford. "That you told the murderer's mother where he was to hang?"

"Wait a minute!" Linda Chambers snarled. "He said it again—at Millertown. Yelled it at the top of his damn voice. The Mexican heard it, but so did everyone else in town."

"Lawman included!" Amelia Finn added.

Mrs. Salisbury's expression became harsher. An angry murmuring started on one sidewalk, reached the group of mounted women and spread along the opposite side of the street.

"I figure they'll be buildin' an extra gallows, Charlie," Webb said, and added a hollow laugh.

"It don't help us," Pike repeated, more dejected than ever.

The widow of the druggist looked as if she was about to spit. But she controlled the impulse. "Get off your horses! All three of you!"

"I reckon you aren't in a listening mood, ladies," Steele said, as he complied with the order.

"Our mood ain't changed from the time you said you'd help us, Steele!" Amy Richards called bitterly.

The hands of Pike and Webb had to be cut loose from their saddle horns. Mrs. Salisbury waited impatiently for this to be done. Then ordered Joan Ricter and two other Winchester-toting women to escort the prisoners to the courthouse cells.

As Steele walked between the two other men along Main Street, he saw only one face which was not emanating hatred toward him. For Julia King was expressing a kind of injured noncomprehension.

Mrs. Salisbury beckoned for Amelia Finn and Linda Chambers to follow her and spun on her heels to head back for the drugstore.

The mounted women wheeled their horses to the side, opening up a passage for the prisoners and escorts to swing between the church and the bank and start across Mine Road toward the impressive courthouse building.

On Main Street, the women gathered into a tight-knit group in front of the drugstore.

"Whose side you on, Steele?" Matt Webb rasped as they were herded along the side of the courthouse and into a doorway at the rear.

"Reckoned to be on the right one for once in my life," the Virginian answered evenly.

"In this case, might makes right!" Mrs. Ricter snarled. "The same way Sherrill and his killers figured it did when they came here that Sunday!"

"And look what's happening to them, ma'am," Steele pointed out.

The doorway gave on to a corridor. There was a plastered wall on one side, featured with wooden doors. Along the other side was a row of six cells, one of them occupied by two men Steele had never seen before and another holding Mitchell and Bergen.

"Wheeler, they got Charlie and Matt!" the youngster groaned, rousing the sleeping Mitchell with a knee in the man's ribs. Both the kid's broken wrists were in slings. "Hey! And that bastard Steele's under the gun!"

The one-eyed man looked sleepily at the newcomers and then glowered at his cellmate. "Don't matter who they got or what they got, Thad. Sherrill'll see nothin' bad happens to us."

The two lawmen, who had been allowed to keep their badges of office, expressed confusion. The woman Steele had taken from O'Ryan's saloon in Carly was on guard in the cell block. There was a sneer of contempt on her no-longer-painted face as she keyed open the doors of two more cells. Webb and Pike were ordered into the one next to their fellow raiders. Steele stepped

127

into the fifth one. The front of each cell was made of an iron grille set with a barred door. The other three walls were of windowless red brick. Thus, the prisoners were unable to see each other.

"We've got to expect more law, Stella," Joan Ricter told the woman from O'Ryan's. "As well as the rest of the Sherrill bunch."

"Gomez knows we're here, you guys," Webb called to Mitchell and Bergen. "Seems the bounty hunter got tired of chasin' us. Figured to set a baited trap."

"Let you know what Margery decides," Mrs. Ricter told Stella, as she and the other two escorts left.

"Decide a friggin' way!" Bergen snarled after them. "Won't nothin' stop Clyde gettin' us out."

"Shut your filthy mouth!" the woman from O'Ryan's yelled at the youngster.

"What if he don't, sister?" Webb taunted. "You gonna spank him on the ass before you hang him?"

He led the other three members of the Sherrill bunch in raucous laughter. The woman from O'Ryan's was still crimson with the fury of frustration as she halted outside Steele's cell.

"Stella what?" the Virginian asked.

He had heard her halt in front of his cell, without seeing her. For he was stretched out on the narrow, uncovered planking of the cot, his hat tipped forward over his face.

"Starrett, if it matters!" she snapped. Then she moderated her tone. "Why did you do it, Steele?"

"Do what?"

"Cross us!" A snarl again.

"Wasn't the intention, ma'am."

The laughter had subsided and there was total silence in the cell block, except when it was punctured by the words of the prisoner and guard.

"What was the intention then?"

"You ever killed anybody, ma'am?"

128

"No, of course not."

"Any of the other women in town ever kill anybody?"

"I should hardly think so."

"That's what I thought. Just reckoned to keep things that way."

"A friggin' knight in friggin' shinin' armor!" Wheeler Mitchell growled.

"You've never been that in your life, Steele!" the woman accused with heavy venom.

"Never claimed it, ma'am," Steele replied wearily.

"There will be no regret after we have hanged the murderers!" Her tone became suspicious. "Or was it Sherrill and his band you were trying to protect? While cheating us out of the money?"

"What money, ma'am?"

He raised the brim of his hat to look out through the bars at her. And saw the bitterness fade from her face to be replaced by confusion. She met his steady gaze for a moment, then shrugged.

"All right. So you acted from a fine motive, Mr. Steele. Perhaps the other women will understand . . . after this is all over. But it will not be over until we have hanged every one of the murderers."

"Fat chance, sister!" Webb spat. "It'll be us who hang you and all the other biddies. The lawmen and friggin' Steele as well."

"You hear that, Steele?" Thadius Bergen taunted. "You're gonna finish up dancin' on the end of a rope!"

The confident tones of the Sherrill Raiders reached Stella Starrett and her eyes expressed fear for a moment. Then the Virginian blotted her out by allowing the hat to fall back over his face.

"I heard, feller," he called evenly. "Seems I may have picked the wrong partners."

129

CHAPTER ELEVEN

It was ten days later—another Sunday evening—when six men approached Borderville from the south. Clyde Sherrill, Manuel Gomez, Tom Kastle, Vince Bowton, Phil Riley and John Slade. They came out of Sonora and into Arizona on foot, dressed entirely in black and with their faces, hands and rifle barrels darkened by dye. They bellied up the final slope of the hill, crested it and crouched in the cover of the gallows.

Below them the town of Borderville was going through its evening routine—following a course of events that had become normal since the widows had come into the possession of prisoners and the knowledge that they could expect trouble from raiders and lawmen alike.

Evening service in the church was over. The Far West Saloon on Main Street and the restaurant on Mine Road were open, but few took advantage of the opportunity to gather in these places. Almost half the women stood guard at strategic points on the fringes of town. Julia King was on duty at the courthouse cell block and Amy Richards and Amelia Finn were serving a meal to the prisoners.

As it had been since the town went onto a state of full alert following Steele's return, a yellow quarantine flag hung at the head of the courthouse pole. Because there was no wind, it was displayed on a bracket and a lamp hung above dropped a cone of light over it.

Until Sherrill and the Mexican began to belly down the hill from under the center gallows platforms, the flag had successfully kept people away from Borderville. Neither the Millertown sheriff nor any other lawman had been among the infrequent would-be visitors who had turned and hurried away on seeing the yellow flag.

It was a bright night, with a full moon and a sky full of glinting stars. The air was cold and still, promising a frost for later.

Sherrill and the Mexican were dressed in warm clothing and the involuntary excitement that was generated by their mission acted to raise their body heat still further.

Fury had been the first response of all the men who heard Gomez's message from Steele. Then had come calm determination as they gathered into the depleted group and rode south for Borderville. Now, even those who held back in the cover of the gallows experienced the same sensations as the two men inching down the slope.

The first raid on the town had been good because it brought back memories of the war. Gave them a taste of excitement and glory that had been missing from the humdrum lives they had all led since the war ended. But the massacre had lacked much which had made the jayhawking days so exhilarating.

But this time it was going to be different.

Each and every one of them felt the thirst for vengeance as keenly as Sherrill. And Sherrill had drawn no lines to this raid. So there would be much more than simple killing. There would be raping and torture, looting and burning. And, when they rode away with the freed prisoners, Borderville and every inhabitant of the town would be wiped off the face of the earth.

And there would be no one left to tell the tale. Except for Sherrill's Raiders, who would go their own peaceful way again—not to talk, but content to merely remember.

"Said it before and I'll say it again, lady," Charlie Pike commented lightly. "Food in this jail just has to be the best served up any place in the country."

He was ignored by the three women out in the corridor, but his comments drew sounds of approval from Webb, Mitchell and Bergen. And it was probably true. The food and general care of the prisoners had been constantly good despite the fact that the strain of waiting was beginning to take its effect on the captors.

The women who either guarded or attended to the needs of the prisoners became more nervous, ill-tempered and sullen with each passing day.

The two marshals—Goring and Brady—were equally ill at ease. They talked little, except to complain to each other at the way they had been fooled by the innocent look of the town when they rode in; had been welcomed with apparent contriteness—only to have Winchesters aimed at them from four directions as they sat down to a meal.

The morale of the four Sherrill's Raiders improved by the same degree that the mood of the women and lawmen got darker.

Adam Steele slept, paced his cell or simply lay on the cot contemplating his situation and resolving to survive. He remained as impassive when awake as when he was asleep. He never once responded to, or even acknowledged, the tacit messages which Julia King directed at him with her eyes. He merely noted them and decided that the girl did not herself know exactly what she was trying to get across to him.

He was asleep when Clyde Sherrill cut the throat of Joan Ricter.

The woman was in the porch of the church and, like her two fellow widows—one standing on a pew and the other in the area under the tower—had been keeping

132

close watch on the hillside topped by the gallows. But they had been watching this piece of terrain, or different stretches on other sides of Borderville, for long periods over the past ten days. They were weary, nervous and bored, wanting too desperately to see the first sign of an attack. And, had Sherrill and Gomez approached fast, the advance would certainly have been spotted.

But the two men took more than an hour to cover the short distance. By moving no more than an inch at a time, they looked like immobile patches of shade, like so many others on the moon-bright hill slope. Had the watchers looked away from the area of surveillance for long periods, they might have noted a change in the formation of the shadow patches. But they never looked away; merely swept their eyes from one side of their field of vision to the other.

Joan Ricter saw her killer's darkened face appear on the outside of the slit window through which she was peering. Her eyes sprang wide and her mouth gaped. Breath rattled up from her throat, but terror silenced the scream of alarm.

Sherrill, his snarling teeth gleaming white against his blackened face, reached a hand through the slit. As he hooked his fingers over the neckline of her dress, she threw her head back and arched her spine in a reflex action. This presented the curve of her throat toward the man. Sherrill's knife hand snaked in—and the blade plunged through the flesh. With a grunt of satisfaction, the man moved his hand to left and right. Blood splashed out over it, as skin and tissue were sliced by the keen double-edge of the knife.

Joan Ricter sighed into death and Sherrill withdrew the killing blade and leaned through the window to lower her limp body to the ground inside the porch.

"Is done, *amigo*?" Gomez whispered rising up alongside Sherrill as the latter came erect.

The leader of the raiders showed the grinning Mexican the blood-stained knife blade. "After you now, Manuel."

The Mexican took the lead, around the side of the porch and into it. Both men glanced along the two streets of Borderville and saw nothing that moved. But they knew from their survey when they reached the hill crest that women were watching for them from secret places.

Inside the church, moonlight streaming through the windows threw many shadows. The two men made use of these, after Sherrill had used hand signals to indicate that Gomez should take the woman under the tower. This meant that the Mexican had further to go, and Sherrill waited patiently between two pews for a sign that the second Borderville widow had died.

Gomez felt his excitement rise as he approached the broad back of the wife of the town's deceased mortician. In his mind was a vivid memory of his own wife's naked body spread upon the marriage bed at the Millertown hotel. And Borderville was truly like the war again, for then a sexual fantasy had always accompanied an act of killing.

He drew his knife, clutched it in both hands, went into a crouch and dropped his forearms between his knees. He had been holding his breath for fifteen seconds. Sweat beads stood out on his leering face. He leaned forward, unfolded his body, then plunged the knife into the base of the broad back.

The sense of another's presence close by caused the woman to start to turn. She had moved hardly at all when the blade penetrated her flesh—just enough to cause the honed steel to miss a vital organ.

"Help!" she thought she screamed. But she had tried too hard and her vocal chords were paralyzed by the strain.

Gomez rasped a curse in his native tongue and jerked out the knife. Blood drenched his hands.

134

The woman standing on the pew heard the faint sounds of the scuffle and the whispered Spanish word. She whirled, reaching for the revolver stuck into the waistband of her dress.

"Shit on you, *amigo*!" Sherrill snarled. He had hoped to take one of the women alive—to use as a hostage in bartering for the release of his four men who were prisoners.

But he could not take a chance on this one getting off a lucky shot. So he hurled the knife as he powered erect from between the pews. She was facing him, the gun drawn and coming up to the aim. The knife sank into her flesh precisely where he had intended it—going in deep to penetrate the heart.

"Help us!" the woman managed to whisper as the revolver dropped from her hand and she went backward to flop out through the slit window.

It was a dying plea to heaven, spoken in God's house. And seemed for a moment to go unheeded. For Sherrill was able to lunge forward and catch the gun before it clattered to the floor.

Under the tower, Manuel Gomez rectified his mistake. He had the knife in both hands still, and stepped to the side as the critically injured woman turned toward him. He crouched, straightened, and drove the blade into the fat woman for a second time. It found the bulbous belly and the shock of the new assault, so fast after the first, killed her. She staggered backward, drawing herself off the blade, hit the wall, and fell forward.

The Mexican was unbalanced after the killing blow. The toppling corpse hit him and sent him reeling. He continued to grasp the knife with one hand. The other one reached for a source of support.

It fisted around a rope, but Manuel Gomez fell to the floor anyway. To the accompaniment of a single *clang*

135

as the bell in the tower responded to the pull on its rope.

Thus, seconds after a dying woman had implored help, the agreed signal for danger was sounded as the result of an action by another dying woman.

"They're coming!" Julia King said hoarsely, her voice sounding very loud in the cell block of the court-house after the single note of the bell.

"Good old Clyde!" Thad Bergen yelled.

Mitchell, Pike and Webb roared their agreement.

"Let us out, lady!" Marshal Brady pleaded.

"Come on, do it!" Goring added urgently. "You women are gonna need all the help you can get."

"Shut up! Shut up! Shut up, all of you!" the pretty, near hysterical young woman ordered, starting along the corridor toward the outside door as rifle fire exploded.

Sherrill's Raiders and the women defenders of Bor-derville responded in their own way to the same signal.

Clyde Sherrill had wanted to keep the attack a secret one until all his men were infiltrated into the town. But he had foreseen the possibility of the alarm being raised before this was achieved. And the four men on the hill crest had their back-up orders. Under covering fire from the furious Sherrill and the abruptly dejected Gomez, they broke from the cover of the gallows and raced down the slope, exploding shots on the run.

For their part, certain of the women held their posi-tions, searching fearfully for signs that the attack was being launched from more than one quarter. Others at-tempted to close in on the church.

Steele had come up off his cot as the bell tolled just once. He heard the excited yells and urgent pleas of his fellow prisoners as he reached the barred door. Then the gunfire and strident voice of Julia King and her fast footfalls against the floor of the corridor. He recalled the many tacit messages she had directed toward him, glimpsed her face as she started across in front of his

136

cell, and recognized the all-consuming fear which contorted her profile.

She had a Colt revolver clutched in her hand, thrust out in front of her. Her wide eyes stared directly ahead of her.

The Virginian raised his right hand to his chest, fisted it around one weighted corner of his scarf, and whipped his hand down. The scarf came clear of the nape of his neck and streaked between two bars of the door.

With the action of a bullwhip, but lacking the crack of leather, the silken material went over and around the barrel of the gun.

A cry of alarm exploded from Julia King's gaping mouth. But she held fast to the Colt as Steele jerked back on the scarf. She was halted in her forward movement, turned, and wrenched toward the cell door. Steele, his youthful looks lost under a mask of grim intent, reached out with his free hand and plucked the gun from the woman's grasp as the scarf fell free.

"They'll hate me!" she cried, lunging back from the cell.

"It's something you learn to live with, ma'am," the Virginian told her, and aimed the Colt at the door lock.

His only concession to the risk of ricochets was to turn his head away as he fired three shots at the lock.

The woman covered her ears with her hands and sprinted along the corridor. She had jerked open the main door and fled out into the night before Steele was free.

"How the hell—?" Charlie Pike started as Steele moved down the corridor.

He and the other three members of the Sherrill bunch stared in fearful amazement as the Virginian swung the scarf back to its accustomed place.

"An old Indian trick," Steele muttered with a sardonic grin.

"Steele?" Brady called.

"I got you into this," Steele answered, reaching for the key to the cells which was hung beside the main door. "Get you out this far." He fitted the key into the lock and turned it. "On your own now, though."

Grinning with relief, the two marshals lunged out of the cell, Goring grabbing the key from the lock and thrusting it into his top pocket.

Steele was outside by then, the crack of rifle and handgun fire loud in his ears and the stink of gunsmoke in his nostrils.

The battle was centered on the church, shots cracking out from the slit windows and being aimed toward them from the facing buildings at the end of Main Street and Mine Road.

Two gowned figures were slumped inertly in the open. Others crouched in cover, rocking with the recoils of their weapons each time they fired a shot.

Steele took in the battle scene at a glance, then raced across the broad Mine Road. The new funeral parlor was completed now. He went around it, discarding the revolver, across the back lot and felt a stab of fear as he reached the wheelless wagon out back of the livery stables. But the two men racing toward him as he whirled were Brady and Goring.

"You got a plan?" Brady asked, panting.

"Just to get my rifle back right now, feller," Steele rasped, and crashed against the rear door of the stable.

It burst open and horses snorted their displeasure at the abruptness of the intrusion. Whatever brand of panic had gripped them at the start of the gunfire had been forgotten.

Steele recognized his gelding in the moonlight and crossed to the stall as the two marshals came into the stable. His gear was hung on a hook outside the stall. The Colt Hartford was in the saddleboot and the knife was stuck in his bedroll.

138

"Hey!" Goring exclaimed gleefully and scuttled across the stable toward another stall as Steele claimed his weapons and delved into a saddlebag for a carton of shells.

"We're in business again!" his partner yelled, as both men retrieved their rifles and gunbelts.

Steele stepped out on to Main Street through the livery's front door. From here, he could see four women slumped on the ground, the dark stains of blood ugly on their gowns. One was scratching at the dust with her fingers, until a bullet from the church powered into her head and exited amid a gout of blood.

The Virginian grimaced, then set his face in impassive lines. Behind him, the two marshals shouted, but he ignored them and sprinted across Main Street. Two bullets cracked close to his head. He ducked into the alley between the saloon and Ricter's Grocery Store. A glance over his shoulder showed him Brady and Goring running out through the rear door of the livery stable.

Since they had become widows the women of Borderville had showed themselves to be as capable as men in most things. But it was probable that not even their menfolk would have been able to survive an attack by Sherrill's Raiders.

Weight of numbers was immaterial. Sherrill and his men were war-trained guerrillas. They fired one shot in exchange for many more exploded by the inexperienced defenders. But each shot from the church was carefully aimed at a known target. Invariably, a woman was killed or wounded. And the man who aimed the shot ducked into cover as wild answering fire was directed in his general direction. Not only ducked into cover, but moved to another position.

Steele heard the gunshots and the screams, the yells of delight and howls of misery. But he could not see the battle as he raced along behind the buildings on the east side of Main Street.

From the rear corner of the manse Steele moved along the side of the building to the front stoop. He crouched there and looked at the church for a full thirty seconds. By then he knew there were just three men firing from inside the building—constantly moving from one slit window to the next so that it appeared there were more.

He sucked in a deep breath, tensed his muscles, and lunged from the manse to the church porch. It was a distance of twenty yards and a fusillade of shots tracked him; from the guns of the women reduced to the state of firing at anything that moved.

He reached the porch and halted on the threshold of the church doorway. His mind raced to consider the possibilities. Only three of Sherrill's Raiders had come to Borderville to rescue their colleagues. Only three were still alive at this stage of the battle. Only three were left in the church while the rest moved deeper into town.

Steele chose to ignore the variables for the moment. He had sought to protect the women from the results of taking the law into their own hands. By their own actions, they had caused him to fail. And by their own actions they were being slaughtered by the same men who had massacred their husbands.

But the actions of the women were immaterial to Steele as he stepped over the inert form of Joan Ricter and into the church. He had caused those of Sherrill's Raiders who were still free to come back to Borderville, as well provided with guns and a thirst for vengeance as they had been on their first raid.

That was all that mattered; his own responsibility. Which he could not load onto the shoulders of women already overburdened with grief.

He shot Phil Riley first, as the man turned from a window to make for another one. The bullet crashed

140

into his chest and sent him into a wild somersault over two pews.

John Slade was next, taking the bullet from the Colt Hartford in the back of his head as he lined up a shot on a woman outside.

Vince Bowton was caught in the act of starting to reload his Winchester. He was furthest away, under the tower where the body of the fat woman was slumped. Moonlight shafting through a window showed his face clearly. And, as he hurled away the rifle and drew his Colt from the holster, his expression revealed that he knew a handgun was not good enough.

He exploded a shot that went high and wide. The response from the smoking muzzle of the Colt Hartford drove a bullet into the center of his forehead. He staggered backward, gushing blood from the wound, and fell against the bell rope. The rope merely swayed without sounding the bell. Bowton slammed to the floor.

The Virginian had remained just inside the church as he made the three shots, turning only the rifle and his head to aim at each target in turn.

Now he lunged into fast movement again, racing for the side aisle and down it. He paused momentarily at each window, to crack a shot through it. Every one was aimed high. Three shots emptied his own rifle and he scooped up Riley's Winchester. Answering fire thudded bullets into the wall of the church. Now and then lead whined in through a window.

He knew that more women would die before the battle for Borderville was over. But there was no alternative if Sherrill's Raiders were to fail in their ultimate aim. It was useless to contemplate what might have been had he approached the bounty hunt differently.

So he continued to move back and forth along the aisle, making use of every gun discarded by the dead men. They were all empty and he had to pause, gasping for breath as he reloaded the Colt Hartford, when the voice of Clyde Sherrill bellowed across the gunfire outside.

"Quit it, you bitches! Hold your damn fire or see the kids die!"

The shooting was abruptly curtailed. In a stretched second of silence, Steele rose in front of a window and peered out at Borderville. A dozen or more bodies were sprawled in the street now. Perhaps there were more dead, crumpled behind cover that had proved inadequate.

He shifted his gaze to look along Mine Road.

Women began to vent their anguish then, with shrill screams that masked their footfalls as they sprinted out of cover.

Clyde Sherrill was advancing along the center of the street. Gomez, Bergen and Kastle were in a line on his right. On his left were Webb, Pike and Mitchell. All the men except the crippled Bergen were armed with Winchesters. Every rifle was aimed toward the group of twenty or more children who sobbed as they moved ahead of the raiders.

Sherrill elevated his rifle an inch and squeezed off a shot. The bullet snatched at a small girl's floppy hat and scaled it from her head. The child screamed, but the women were abruptly silent.

"Drop the guns, bitches!" Sherrill demanded, his handsome face inscribed with a grin of triumph.

"We'll start blastin', you don't do like Clyde tells you!" Bergen threatened.

There had been more than fifty women before the raiders attacked. Less than thirty allowed rifles and revolvers to slip from their quaking hands. Without being told to, they scuttled away from the discarded weapons to gather in the close-knit group at the lower end of Mine Road.

"Go to your mommies, kids!" Sherrill yelled.

Steele was midway up the stairs which led to the top of the short tower. He heard the running feet of the children; their sobs and shouts; the shrill voices of mothers calling the names of their children.

Then a volley of rifle shots that again brought silence; not quite complete because some of the younger children were unable to stem their relief or their grief.

The Virginian reached the belfry and looked down. The guns of the raiders were still smoking from the shots that had been exploded high into the air.

"Okay, Vince!" Sherrill yelled. "You and Johnnie and Phil okay? We got them. Come on out and join the fun."

Then he and the others advanced on the terrified group of Borderville citizens, mothers clasping their own children and the orphans to their dirt- and blood-streaked gowns. They knew there were more women than the raiders needed. Desperation was stark on every face. Was it better to be shot now, rather than to endure the rape and torture that it was obvious the raiders intended? But what about the children? What would happen to them? Surely even Sherrill's Raiders would not . . .

"Steele?" Stella Starrett shrieked from the center of the terror-stricken huddle.

Bergen laughed.

"That coward has run, *señoras*!" Gomez taunted. "We hear this from the lips of the lawmen before we slit their throats! Just as the *hombre* ran from me on my wedding night!"

"A lesson learned too late!" Sherrill snarled. "Never set a chicken to catch dogs of war."

Steele eased out on to the ledge around the belfry, knowing he was making himself a clear target—the dark of his clothing contrasting with the moonlight-bathed whiteness of the adobe tower. He pushed the stock plate of the Colt Hartford against his right shoulder, drew a bead on Sherrill's chest—and squeezed the trigger.

A man who had contributed to the jayhawking legend of Bloody Kansas flipped over backward and poured his own blood on to the soil of Arizona.

Gomez was a corpse and falling before Sherrill's twitching nerves were stilled by death. Another heart shot.

Mitchell was hit next, taking the bullet in the side of the neck as he swung his head to look toward the dead men.

Kastle, Pike and Webb vented curses and fired at the figure in the church tower. But they were moving, lunging for cover.

Chips of adobe spat into Steele's face. He did not alter his impassive expression.

A fourth shot from the Colt Hartford went into Webb's shoulder, scraped a bone but had enough velocity to reach the heart.

The women broke from the group, screaming as they scattered, plucking children from the ground or dragging them through the dust.

Steele felt a blow against his right thigh, then the warmth of flowing blood. His legs continued to support him. The recoil of the Colt Hartford thudded the stock plate against his shoulder as he fired a shot into the back of Tom Kastle.

Charlie Pike reached the side of the new funeral parlor, diving into its cover in the wake of the unarmed Thadius Bergen. The final bullet from Steele's rifle exploded splinters of new wood from the building.

But Pike screamed and staggered back onto the open street, both hands clutched to his face. Blood squeezed between his clawed fingers. He dropped to his knees, his arms fell to his side and he showed a blood-streaming eye socket before he tipped forward and was still.

Steele remained where he was, feeling a weakness in his right leg.

The women stopped running and stared toward the funeral parlor.

Bergen backed into sight, his mouth flapping but no words coming out.

Julia King tracked him, covering him with a revolver in a two-handed grip. When the young woman came to a halt, so did Bergen.

A small girl was crying. It was the only sound in Borderville.

"The church!" Stella Starrett cried. "The men in the church?"

Julia King continued to stare at the cowering Bergen as every other woman turned to gaze fearfully up at Steele.

"Somebody said a while back you were a gallows short, ladies," the Virginian called down, tucking the Colt Hartford under his arm and starting to pull off his gloves. "Seems you got the full nine too many."

145

CHAPTER TWELVE

Adam Steele watched while the women worked. Nobody had helped him down from the bell tower. But nobody tried to prevent him from using the facilities of the drugstore and the hotel to treat his flesh wound and then wash up. He took his time over the chores, for he did not intend to leave Borderville until dawn. By the time he emerged on to Main Street again, sore and limping but certain the wound was not serious, the work of the women was well under way.

The town's dead, plus the corpses of the marshals Brady and Goring, were stacked in the new funeral parlor. Kerosene-soaked hay bales were being built around it. A cross was being made, identical to the one already set up to the right of the courthouse steps. Bullet holes were being filled in, smashed windows replaced, and blood stains washed away. Where possible, the women worked in silence. Sometimes, the voice of Thadius Bergen could be heard, calling plaintively for his mother or screaming abuse at the dead Clyde Sherrill.

If any woman happened to glance at Steele, there was in her empty eyes a look which suggested she could not see him. After a while, he went up to one of the rooms in the Far West Saloon and stretched out on the bed.

A smell of burning disturbed his sleep once and he saw that the pre-dawn sky was filled with an orange glow. His sense of smell told him what was on fire.

He had a dream of envying the sheriff of Millertown;

146

relishing the prospect of being able to ignore everything which happened beyond an arbitrary jurisdiction.

The clanging of the church bell roused him as the first rays of the new sun shafted across the eastern horizon. A man's voice called out between deep sobs, but it was too hoarse for the words to be understood.

Steele went downstairs, across Main Street and into the livery stable. The bell continued to ring out as he saddled the gelding, led the animal outside and mounted him.

The town, which still smelled of roasted meat, was deserted. Not so the crest of the hill to the south.

All the women were up there, with their own children and the new orphans. Most stood on the barren slope. Ten were in position on the gallows platforms, hands on the trap levers. In the bright sunlight of early morning, the Virginian recognized Stella Starrett, Margery Salisbury and Julia King, their faces deathly pale against the black of their mourning gowns. The rest of the women he knew only by sight.

Margery Salisbury was the only executioner proper. She was to hang the sobbing and trembling Thadius Bergen. The other nine nooses were around the necks of men already dead.

"Lord, we ask forgiveness for what we are about to do!" Mrs. Salisbury pleaded, turning her face heavenward. "But we have suffered much and crave Thy divine indulgence in our need to claim vengeance. And we ask you to have mercy on the living and the souls of the dead, even those who brought death to our town."

While the other women continued to turn their faces to the sky, their hands clasped and their eyes tightly shut, Margery Salisbury stared down at the mounted Steele.

"Forgive us all, oh Lord!" she went on, her voice shrill and clear in the still cold air of morning.

The prayer had been rehearsed. In unison, the

147

women on the gallows wrenched over the levers. Thadius Bergen screamed once more for his mother, and vomited. Nine corpses and one living man dropped through the trap-door openings. The youngster spasmed once and then became as limp as the bullet-shattered dead.

". . . for we are only human and know not what we do!" Mrs. Salisbury finished, still gazing down at Steele.

"Nor why we do it," the Virginian muttered, and touched the brim of his hat as he slowly wheeled his horse.

"Amen!" the women and children on the hill crest chorused reverently.

Steele pursed his lips. "Reckon that's . . . the last word."

Out of the American West rides a new hero.
He rides alone . . . trusting no one.

SPECIAL PREVIEW

Edge *is not like other western novels. In a tradition-bound
genre long dominated by the heroic cowpoke, we now have
the western anti-hero, an un-hero . . . a character seemingly
devoid of any sympathetic virtues. "A mean, sub-bitchin,'
baad-ass!" For readers who were introduced to the western via
Fran Striker's Lone Ranger tales, and who have learned about
the ways of the American West from the countless volumes
penned by Max Brand and Zane Grey, the adventures of* Edge
*will be quite shocking. Without question, these are the most
violent and bloody stories ever written in this field. Only two
things are certain about* Edge: *first, he is totally unpredicta-
ble, and has no pretense of ethics or honor . . . for him there
is no Code of the West, no Rules of the Range. Secondly, since
the first book of* Edge's *adventures was published by Pinnacle
in July of 1972, the sales and reader reaction have continued
to grow steadily.* Edge *is now a major part of the western
genre, alongside ol' Max and Zane, and Louis L'Amour. But*

Edge *will never be confused with any of 'em, because* Edge *is an original, tough hombre who defies any attempt to be cleaned up, calmed-down or made honorable. And who is to say that* Edge *may not be a realistic portrayal of our early American West? Perhaps more authentic than we know.*

George G. Gilman created *Edge* in 1971. The idea grew out of an editorial meeting in a London pub. It was, obviously, a fortunate blending of concepts between writer and editor. Up to this point Mr. Gilman's career included stints as a newspaperman, short story writer, compiler of crossword puzzles, and a few not-too-successful mysteries and police novels. With the publication in England of his first *Edge* novel, *The Loner*, Mr. Gilman's writing career took off. British readers went crazy over them, likening them to the "spaghetti westerns" of Clint Eastwood. In October, 1971, an American editor visiting the offices of New English Library in London spotted the cover of the first book on a bulletin board and asked about it. He was told it was "A cheeky Britisher's incredibly gory attempt at developing a new western series." Within a few days Pinnacle's editor had bought the series for publication in the United States. "It was," he said, "the perfect answer to the staid old westerns, which are so dull, so predictable, and so all-alike."

The first reactions to *Edge* in New York were incredulous. "Too violent!" "It's too far from the western formula, fans won't accept it." "How the hell can a British writer write about *our* American West?" But Pinnacle's editors felt they had something hot, and that the reading public was ready for it. So they published the first two *Edge* books simultaneously; *The Loner* and *Ten Grand* were issued in July 1972.

But, just *who* is Edge? We'll try to explain. His name was Josiah Hedges, a rather nondescript, even innocent, monicker for the times. Actually we meet Josiah's younger brother, Jamie Hedges, first. It is 1865, in the state of Iowa, a peaceful farmstead. The Civil War is over and young Jamie is awaiting the return of his brother, who's been five years at war. Six hundred thousand others have died, but Josiah was coming home. All would be well again. Jamie could hardly contain his excitement. He wasn't yet nineteen.

The following is an edited version of the first few chapters, as we are introduced to Josiah Hedges:

* * *

Six riders appeared in the distance, it must be Josiah! But then Jamie saw something which clouded his face, caused him to reach down and press Patch's head against his leg, giving or seeking assurance.

"Hi there, boy, you must be Joe's little brother Jamie."

He was big and mean-looking and, even though he smiled as he spoke, his crooked and tobacco-browned teeth gave his face an evil cast. But Jamie was old enough to know not to trust first impressions: and the mention of his brother's name raised the flames of excitement again.

"You know Joe? I'm expecting him. Where is he?"

"Well, boy," he drawled, shuffling his feet. "Hell, when you got bad news to give, tell it quick is how I look at things. Joe won't be coming today. Not any day. He's dead, boy."

"We didn't only come to give you the news, boy," the sergeant said. "Hardly like to bring up another matter, but you're almost a man now. Probably are a man in everything except years—living out here alone in the wilderness like you do. It's money, boy.

"Joe died in debt, you see. He didn't play much poker, but when he did there was just no stopping him."

Liar, Jamie wanted to scream at them. *Filthy rotten liar.*

"Night before he died," the sergeant continued. "Joe owed me five hundred dollars. He wanted to play me double or nothing. I didn't want to, but your brother was sure a stubborn cuss when he wanted to be."

Joe never gambled. Ma and Pa taught us both good.

"So we played a hand and Joe was unlucky." His gaze continued to be locked on Jamie's, while his discolored teeth were shown in another parody of a smile. "I wasn't worried none about the debt, boy. See, Joe told me he'd been sending money home to you regular like."

"There ain't no money on the place and you're a lying son-ofabitch. Joe never gambled. Every cent he earned went into a bank so we could do things with this place. Big things. I don't even believe Joe's dead. Get off our land."

Jamie was held erect against this oak, secured by a length of rope that bound him tightly at ankles, thighs, stomach, chest, and throat; except for his right arm left free of the bonds so that it could be raised out and the hand fastened, fingers splayed over the tree trunk by nails driven between them and bent over. But Jamie gritted his teeth and looked back at Forrest defiantly, trying desperately to conceal the twisted terror that reached his very nerve ends.

"You got your fingers and a thumb on that right hand, boy," Forrest said softly. "You also got another hand and we got lots of nails. I'll start with the thumb. I'm good. That's why they made me platoon sergeant. Your brother recommended me, boy. I don't miss. Where's the money?"

The enormous gun roared and Jamie could no longer feel anything in his right hand. But Forrest's aim was true and when the boy looked down it was just his thumb that lay in the dust, the shattered bone gleaming white against the scarlet blood pumping from the still warm flesh. Then the numbness went and white hot pain engulfed his entire arm as he screamed.

"You tell me where the money is hid, boy," Forrest said, having to raise his voice and make himself heard above the sounds of agony, but still empty of emotion.

The gun exploded into sound again and this time there was no moment of numbness as Jamie's forefinger fell to the ground.

"Don't hog it all yourself, Frank," Billy Seward shouted, drawing his revolver. "You weren't the only crack shot in the whole damn war."

"You stupid bastard," Forrest yelled as he spun around. "Don't kill him. . . ."

But the man with the whiskey bottle suddenly fired from the hip, the bullet whining past Forrest's shoulder to hit Jamie squarely between the eyes, the blood spurting from the fatal wound like red mud to mask the boy's death agony. The gasps of the other men told Forrest it was over and his Colt spoke again, the bullet smashing into the drunken man's groin. He went down hard into a sitting position, dropping his gun, splaying his legs, his hands clenching at his lower abdomen.

"Help me, Frank, my guts are running out. I didn't mean to kill him."

"But you did," Forrest said, spat full into his face and brought up his foot to kick the injured man savagely on the jaw, sending him sprawling on to his back. He looked around at the others as, their faces depicting fear, they holstered their guns. "Burn the place to the ground," he ordered with low-key fury. "If we can't get the money, Captain damn Josiah C. Hedges ain't gonna find it, either."

Joe caught his first sight of the farm and was sure it was a trick of his imagination that painted the picture hanging before his eyes. But then the gentle breeze that had been coming from the south suddenly veered and he caught the acrid stench of smoke in his nostrils, confirming that the black smudges rising lazily upwards from the wide area of darkened country ahead was actual evidence of a fire.

As he galloped toward what was now the charred remains of the Hedges farmstead, Joe looked down at the rail, recognizing in the thick dust of a long hot summer signs of the recent passage of many horses—horses with shod hoofs. As he thundered up the final length of the trail, Joe saw only two areas of movement, one around the big oak and another some yards distant, toward the smouldering ruins of the house, and as he reined his horse at the gateway he slid the twelve shot Henry repeater from its boot and leapt to the ground, firing from hip level. Only one of the evil buzz that had been tearing ferociously at dead human flesh escaped, lumbering with incensed screeches into the acrid air.

For perhaps a minute Joe stood unmoving, looking at Jamie bound to the tree. He knew it was his brother, even though his face was unrecognizable where the scavengers had ripped the flesh to the bone. He saw the right hand picked almost completely clean of flesh, as a three fingered skeleton of what it had been, still securely nailed to the tree. He took hold of Jamie's shirt front and ripped it, pressed his lips against the cold, waxy flesh of his brother's chest, letting his grief escape, not moving until his throat was pained by dry sobs and his tears were exhausted. . . .

"Jamie, our ma and pa taught us a lot out of the Good Book, but it's a long time since I felt the need to know about such things. I guess you'd know better than me what to say at a time like this. Rest easy, brother, I'll settle your score. Whoever they are and wherever they run, I'll find them and I'll kill them. I've learned some special ways of killing people and I'll avenge you good." Now Joe looked up at the sky, a bright sheet of azure cleared of smoke. "Take care of my kid brother, Lord," he said softly, and put on his hat with a gesture of finality, marking the end of his moments of graveside reverence. Then he went to the pile of blackened timber, which was the corner of what had been Jamie's bedroom. Joe used the edge of the spade to prise up the scorched floor boards. Beneath was a tin box containing every cent of the two thousand dollars Joe had sent home from the war, stacked neatly in piles of one, five, and ten dollar bills.

Only now, more than two hours since he had returned to the farmstead, did Joe cross to look at the second dead man.

The scavenging birds had again made their feast at the man-made source of blood. The dead man lay on his back, arms and legs splayed. Above the waist and below the thighs he was unmarked, the birds content to tear away his genitals and rip a gaping hole in his stomach, their talons and bills delving inside to drag out the intestines, the uneaten portions of which now trailed in the dust. . . .

Then Joe looked at the face of the dead man and his cold eyes narrowed. The man was Bob Rhett, he recalled. He had fought a drunken coward's war, his many failings covered by his platoon sergeant Frank Forrest. So they were the five men who must die . . . Frank Forrest, Billy Seward, John Scott, Hal Douglas, and Roger Bell. They were inseparable throughout the war.

Joe walked to his horse and mounted. He had not gone fifty yards before he saw a buzzard swoop down and tug at something that suddenly came free. Then it rose into the air with an ungainly flapping of wings, to find a safer place to enjoy its prize. As it wheeled away, Joe saw that swinging from its bill were the entrails of Bob Rhett.

Joe grinned for the first time that day, an expression of cold slit eyes and bared teeth that utterly lacked humor. "You never did have any guts, Rhett," he said aloud.

* * *

From this day of horror Josiah Hedges forged a new career as a killer. A killer of the worst kind, born of violence, driven by revenge. As you'll note in the preceding material, Edge often shows his grim sense of irony, a graveyard humor. Edge is not like anyone you've met in fact or fiction. He is without doubt the most cold-bloodedly violent character to ever roam the West. You'll hate him, you'll cringe at what he does, you'll wince at the explicit description of all that transpires . . . and you'll come back for more.